THE
TRAILSMAN
#192

DURANGO
DUEL

by

Jon Sharpe

D0189695

A SIGNET BOOK

SIGNET
Published by the Penguin Group
Penguin Putnam Inc., 375 Hudson Street,
New York, New York 10014, U.S.A.
Penguin Books Ltd, 27 Wrights Lane,
London W8 5TZ, England
Penguin Books Australia Ltd,
Ringwood, Victoria, Australia
Penguin Books Canada Ltd, 10 Alcorn Avenue,
Toronto, Ontario, Canada M4V 3B2
Penguin Books (N.Z.) Ltd, 182–190 Wairau Road,
Auckland 10, New Zealand

Penguin Books Ltd, Registered Offices:
Harmondsworth, Middlesex, England

First published by Signet, an imprint of Dutton Signet,
a member of Penguin Putnam Inc.

First Printing, December, 1997
10 9 8 7 6 5 4 3 2 1

TRUST

Skye Fargo stood beside the Durango Kid, facing Lopez and Ramon, the two *pistoleros* who had come into the saloon.

"Get out of the way, gringo," Lopez told Fargo. "This does not concern you."

Fargo took a casual step to the right so he was directly in front of Ramon. "You've come a long way just to die," Skye said.

Fargo dared not take his eyes off Ramon to check on the Kid. He could only hope that the Kid's reputation was for real. Because these two *pistoleros* were the best money could buy—and Skye could take out only one of them.

The very instant that Ramon's hands dipped, so did Skye's. A heavy slug smashed into Ramon's chest and jolted him backward, but he did not go down. The killer was forged of iron. Fargo fired again. Ramon staggered but tried to level his pistols. Fargo put a third slug into him, and the *pistolero* oozed to the floor like a lump of human wax.

Skye was dimly aware that bullets had been flying beside him. The Durango Kid had better be still on his feet—or else the Trailsman had won his last gunfight. . . .

The Trailsman

Beginnings . . . they bend the tree and they mark the man. Skye Fargo was born when he was eighteen. Terror was his midwife, vengeance his first cry. Killing spawned Skye Fargo, ruthless, cold-blooded murder. Out of the acrid smoke of gunpowder still hanging in the air, he rose, cried out a promise never forgotten.

The Trailsman they began to call him all across the West: searcher, scout, hunter, the man who could see where others only looked, his skills for hire but not his soul, the man who lived each day to the fullest, yet trailed each tomorrow. Skye Fargo, the Trailsman, and the seeker who could take the wildness of a land and the wanting of a woman and make them his own.

1860, the San Juan Mountains,
where hatred and bigotry ignited
a wildfire of violence . . .

1

Skye Fargo heard shouts long before he spotted the frantic man who was doing all the yelling. Reining up in the shadow of an arroyo wall, Fargo studied the situation through narrowed lake-blue eyes. In the wilderness it didn't pay for a lone traveler to take needless risks.

Across a barren stretch of baked landscape rode a skinny man on an old bay. The rider was as long in the tooth as the horse. Gray, unkempt hair spilled from under a beaver hat that had been in its prime when Fargo was sill knee-high to a calf. Grimy, worn buckskins clothed the scarecrow. A possibles bag hung over a scrawny shoulder. Crisscrossing the man's chest were an ammo pouch and a powder horn.

Fargo pegged the old-timer as a mountain man, one of the few of that hardy breed still alive and kicking. During their heyday, they had roamed the high country from Canada to New Mexico, masters of their domain. Most had wound up being killed by hostile Indians or mauled to death by savage beasts. Of the many hundreds who called the mountains home a few short decades ago, only a handful lived on to enjoy the luxury of old age. The smart ones, like Jim Bridger, were whittling their final days away on rocking chairs back East.

This particular old-timer was in a frenzy of anxiety. Constantly glancing to the right and left, again and again he rose in the stirrups to cup a hand to his mouth and bellow, "Clarice! Clarice!" He was nearly hoarse. His face had grown as red as a beet. Drawing rein, the man mopped his sweaty brow with a sleeve, then bowed his head and clutched his throat, choked by deep sorrow.

Judging him to pose no threat, Fargo kneed the Ovaro into the open. No sooner did he do so, however, than the mountain man jerked erect as if prodded by the tip of a Bowie and swung around, leveling an old Hawken.

"Hold on there, mister," Fargo said, holding his hands out from his sides to show he was unarmed. "I'm not out to scalp you."

The old-timer was not amused. Wheeling the bay, he warily approached, his thumb on the Hawken's hammer. Blood lust burned in his dark eyes, leading Fargo to wonder if maybe the man were sunstruck, or just plain loco. "Where is she, damn you?" the old-timer demanded. "What have you done with poor Clarice?"

"The last woman I knew by that name was a dove down in the Staked Plain country of Texas," Fargo mentioned good-naturedly. "She was partial to soft beds and fine whiskey. You'd never catch her in godforsaken territory like this."

The old man did not seem to hear. Curling back the Hawken's hammer, he spat out, "I won't ask you again, sidewinder. Either fess up, or I'll blow a hole in you the size of a melon."

At the distinct click, Fargo stiffened. It was no idle threat. It appeared he had badly misjudged. His right hand slowly started to drop toward the Colt nestled in the holster on his hip. He had no desire to kill the old-timer, but he was not about to sit there and be turned into worm food for no other reason than a vagrant whim of fickle fate. "Listen, you old coot," he said testily, "I've been on the trail for over a week. You're the first person I've seen in eight whole days. I haven't met up with your Clarice. And if I had, I sure as blazes wouldn't hurt her."

The mountain man gnawed on his lower lip, unsure of himself.

Fargo pressed his advantage. Mustering a lopsided grin, he said, "Truth is, I'm fond of the fillies. You could say they're a hobby of mine." He thought that the assurance would calm the old-timer even more, so he was doubly bewildered when the man glowered and hiked the Hawken to his shoulder.

"You stinking coyote. You'd trifle with a girl her age? Why, Clarice ain't but nineteen years old. She's the sweetest, kindest thing on two legs. As pure as the driven snow, that child. To think of you and her—!" The mountain man choked off in stifled outrage and put his grizzled cheek to the Hawken's stock. "I know just where to shoot a no-account critter like you." The Hawken's barrel lowered until the muzzle was fixed on a spot slightly above and behind Fargo's saddle horn.

Goose bumps crawled over Fargo's skin. Of all the places to be shot, *there* was the last part of the male anatomy any man ever wanted to lose. He watched the old-timer's craggy face, alert for a telltale clue that the man was about to fire. His right hand dipped another inch. In the strained silence, the buzzing of a fly sounded unnaturally loud. "You're making a mistake," were his final words on the issue. Whether one or both of them lived or died depended on what the mountain man did next.

Jaw muscles twitching, the old-timer was on the verge of firing when a strident scream to the northwest made him go as rigid as a board. It was the scream of a woman in mortal terror. "Clarice!" the mountain man roared. "Hold on, gal! Hold on! Ol' Lucas is a-coming!"

Tugging on his reins, Lucas spurred the tired old bay into a gallop, racing like a madman toward the mouth of a canyon several hundred yards away. His spindly arms and legs flapped like the wings of a disjointed crow.

Skye Fargo frowned. He was of half a mind to ride off and let the old cuss handle it alone. The man hadn't asked for help. But a woman was involved, a woman in danger. His conscience pricked him into following. The pinto stallion rapidly overtook the bay, and shoulder to shoulder they pounded into the canyon. A basking lizard scuttled out of their way. Sandstone heights loomed. The clatter of flying hooves on stone pealed loudly, the echoes rolling into the distance.

Fargo's frown deepened. They were making so much

noise that whoever was up there with the young woman would hear them, and be ready. Instead of unlimbering the Colt, he yanked his Henry from the boot. The rifle held fifteen shells, more than twice that of the revolver. Its brass receiver and metal barrel gleamed brightly in the sunshine as he worked the lever, inserting a cartridge into the chamber.

Soon a bend appeared. From around it rose another wavering scream, carried by a gust of hot wind. Lucas uttered a wild cry and flagged the lathered bay to go faster, but the old horse was doing the best it could.

Not so the Ovaro. A tap of the rowels on Fargo's spurs, and the big stallion fairly flew around the turn. Fargo raised the Henry, not knowing what to expect, but wanting to be ready for anything. His hunch was that the woman had stumbled on a roving band of Utes. There had been friction of late between the tribe and the ever-growing number of white settlers who were claiming the fertile lowlands and best mountain tracts for their own. As yet, no blood had been spilled. It was only a matter of time, though. Fargo had seen the same pattern play itself out time and again, and it always ended with the Indians being forced to give up their land or pay a fatal price.

But the cause of the woman's screams had nothing to do with the Utes. As Fargo sped around the corner, a rumbling snarl fell on his ears. Almost too late, he saw the enormous creature that barred his path. He reined up in a spray of dust. Fifteen feet away, a shaggy monster reared onto its hind legs, lips curling back over tapered teeth that could rend flesh to the bone in the blink of an eye. The stallion whinnied and shied, as well it might.

"Grizzly!" Fargo hollered, to warn Lucas. It did no good. Passing the Ovaro, Lucas veered to the right to go around the gigantic bear. Unfortunately, large boulders littered the ground on that side. There was not much room for Lucas to get by. A huge paw flicked out with deceptive speed and caught the old-timer across the chest. Lucas was lifted from his saddle and propelled through the air as if shot from a catapult.

Fargo took a hasty bead, but not at the bear. A single shot rarely dispatched grizzlies. They were notoriously hard to kill, even when vital organs were pierced. He would rather drive it off if he could. To that end, he yelled, "Get out of here!" and banged a slug into the ground in front of it.

The bear ignored him. It was more interested in the bay, which had gone on by and was barreling up the canyon in fear for its life. Pivoting ponderously, the grizzly gave chase, its massive muscles rippling. For something so large, it could move quickly when the need arose.

Fargo vaulted off the stallion and sprang to Lucas, who lay in a miserable crumpled heap. Unconscious, Lucas breathed raggedly, unevenly. Scarlet drops flecked the mountain man's lips. Fargo shook him gently, and the old-timer's eyelids fluttered, but did not open.

"Grandpa!"

In the excitement of the moment, Fargo had practically forgotten about Clarice. Turning, he saw her perched on a narrow shelf ten feet above the canyon floor. For the second time in less than a minute, he was surprised by what he beheld.

She was a full-figured lovely in a faded blue cotton dress that clung to her ample bosom and shapely legs as if molded to her form. Lustrous hair the hue of a blazing sunset cascaded below slender shoulders. Eyes the color of sparkling emeralds were wide with concern for the man sprawled beside Fargo. Bending, she scrambled down from her roost with the agility of a mountain sheep. Her dress swirled, showing silken thighs. Lithe and graceful in motion, Clarice was the sort of woman who set a man's heart to thumping. Fargo was so taken aback by her beauty that he did not reply right away when she asked, "How is he, mister?"

A lusty roar from up the canyon diverted their attention. The weary bay had blundered into a pocket in the canyon wall. The horse was barely visible, cowering as the grizzly moved in for the kill.

"Jezebel!" Clarice cried. "Mister, you've got to help her!"

Fargo's boots seemed to move of their own accord. He was on the Ovaro and reining around before the echoes of the shout died out. To discourage the bear, he fired a shot above it. The bullet spanged off rock, chips flying. The grizzly paused to look back, broad head lowered, a study in raw defiance. Fargo fired again, with no result. The hungry brute was not about to be scared off.

The bay was old, but not stupid. With the bear looking the other way, it bolted, fleeing out of the pocket and on up the canyon.

Venting a growl of frustration, the grizzly pursued it. On open ground the horse could easily outdistance the behemoth. Here, twists and turns slowed the horse down. Quarry and predator were only yards apart when they flashed around another bend and were lost to view.

Fargo stopped, then brought the stallion around. The bay was on its own. He had to get the old-timer and the woman out of there.

Clarice was bent low over Lucas, tears staining her perfect cheeks. She glanced up, mute appeal etching her finely chiseled features. "He's in a bad way, mister. We have to get him to the settlement. Doc Carver can help him, if anyone can."

"What settlement?" Fargo responded. The last time he had been through that area, farms and ranches had been springing up, but no established communities had taken root.

"Animas City, folks are calling it," Clarice said. Rising, she snatched at his arm. "Don't just sit there jawing. Hurry. If anything happens to my grandpa, I don't know what I'd do."

Fargo was reluctant to move Lucas without examining him. Odds were, the mountain man was busted up inside. Moving him might make it worse. Maybe kill him, in fact. "We should check for broken bones," Fargo suggested, dismounting. Hunkering, he carefully probed Lucas's limbs

14

and chest. A lower rib yielded to his touch, a clue that at least one was indeed fractured.

"Hurry!" Clarice pleaded.

Added incentive was provided by the grizzly. A series of snorts alerted Fargo to the bear's return. It had rounded the bend and was heading straight for them. Apparently the bay had escaped, so the beast was after other morsels.

"Do you have a horse nearby?" Fargo asked hopefully. Riding double, they had a fair-to-middling chance of escaping. Burdened with Lucas's extra weight, not even the sturdy stallion could pull their fat out of the proverbial fire.

"A mare," Clarice said. "The bear spooked her. She threw me and ran off when it jumped us."

By now the monster was sixty feet away and narrowing the gap at a measured, lumbering gait. Either it was tuckered out from chasing the bay, or it considered them easy prey, because it was no great haste. Which bought them precious extra seconds.

Fargo grabbed Clarice's wrist and spun her toward the Ovaro. "Up you go." Placing his hands on her slim hips, he boosted her into the saddle. Next he slid his arms under Lucas's and hoisted the older man on the stallion belly-down, behind the saddle. It wouldn't help the rib any, but it couldn't be helped. "You'll have to hold him tight."

"Wait a minute. What about you?" Her gorgeous emerald eyes filled with insight, and she gripped his shoulder. "We can't leave you here. That wouldn't be right."

The grizzly was fifty feet off. Fargo shrugged free, stepped to the pinto's flank, and gave the animal a resounding smack. "I'll see you in Animas City later," he called out as Clarice and her grandfather were borne to safety. He stared after them a few moments. Despite his predicament, he could not help but admire how her magnificent mane was whipped by the wind, and how her long, winsome legs clung to the Ovaro.

A growl reminded Fargo that he should keep his mind on the matter at hand. Rotating, he brought up the Henry. The bear was twenty feet from him, just standing there, glaring. He sighted on a point at the base of its throat. The thick skull was impervious, a heart shot out of the question. Scalp prickling, he braced for the furious charge sure to come. If he was lucky, he would get off one shot, perhaps two. Each must count.

The grizzly made no attempt to attack. Lifting its black nose high, it sniffed loudly a few times. Then it cocked its head and regarded the Trailsman intently. What was going through its brain was impossible to gauge. All bears were highly unpredictable. Temperamental by nature, where one might attack at the mere sight of a human, another might run off squalling.

Fargo waited, his finger lightly touching the Henry's trigger. When the grizzly took a shuffling stride toward him, he held his breath to steady his aim. Another step, and he would shoot. He held no illusions about the outcome. The bear would reach him, that much was certain. How much harm it did depended on whether either of his shots ultimately proved fatal—and how long he could stay out of its reach while the lead took effect.

Abruptly, a strange thing happened. From the canyon rim wafted the sound of someone whistling a bawdy song popular in saloons and taverns from the Mississippi River to the Pacific Ocean. The bear looked up, and so did Fargo. Silhouetted against the blue vault of sky was a figure on horseback. Rider and mount were no more than vague black shapes, although the outline of the man's hat suggested he wore a sombrero.

The sight unnerved the bear. Snorting, it turned and ran deeper into the canyon. Every ten yards or so it would peer upward. At the bend, it halted to give voice to a thunderous roar. With that, it was gone.

Fargo exhaled and craned his neck for a better glimpse of his benefactor. The rider raised an arm as if in salute, so he did the same. Man and horse disappeared, the whistling faded. Whoever it was, Fargo reasoned, was bound to ride on down. But minutes elapsed, and no one showed up. Not knowing what to make of the incident, Fargo shouldered the Henry and headed toward the canyon mouth. His spurs jangled softly. Overhead a hawk circled, lost interest, and soared off.

Once in the open, Fargo scanned the vicinity for sign of Clarice. Tendrils of dust to the east marked the direction she had taken. To the north were the blue-green foothills to the La Plata range. Beyond reared stark peaks, some crowned with snow. Far to the northeast were more majestic summits, those of the San Juans. By rights, the grizzly should have been up in the mountains, not prowling the arid lowlands. Occasionally, the big bears wandered down low, proving a menace to settlers and Utes alike.

The sun baked the ground, and Fargo as well. He had not gone half a mile before his buckskins clung to him like a second skin. Pulling his hat brim low, he licked his dry lips. By his reckoning, it was six or seven miles yet to the Animas River. A mighty long way to go when the temperature hovered at one hundred degrees, or better. He shut the heat and discomfort from his mind and thought of pleasant pastimes: the last big poker pot he had won, the last woman he had bedded, that last whiskey he'd savored before hitting the trail.

It was peculiar how people always took what life had to offer for granted, Fargo mused. Only when they were denied the simple pleasures did they truly miss them. He was no exception. When he reached Animas City, he intended to drown himself in rotgut, play stud poker until he was too blurry-eyed to see the cards, and treat himself to a frisky time with the prettiest gal he could find—not necessarily in that order.

The parched landscape mocked his thirst. Even in the mountains, water was hard to come by. Few folks in the States realized how dry Colorado Territory was, especially those flocking there to carve a new niche for themselves out of the merciless terrain. Many invested all the money they had in a wagon and implements, then made the arduous journey west, only to lose the shirts on their backs when their crops withered and their stock died. Their livelihood—and their dreams—went up in puffs of dust.

The *clomp* of hooves brought Fargo up short. Turning,

he saw a rider to the north. It was a tall man dressed mostly in gray, wearing a gray sombrero. He suspected it was the same rider who had been on the canyon rim. Now the man was paralleling him, staying just out of rifle range. Who was he? Fargo wondered. What did he want?

Continuing on, Fargo kept one eye on his shadow at all times. The open plain he was crossing offered few places to take shelter, should it come to that. But he was not worried. He had the Henry. If the rider proved to be a threat, he could hold his own. Settling into a long, mile-eating stride, he traveled for another half an hour. Just when he had about convinced himself that the man was not going to do anything, lo and behold, the rider slanted toward him and approached at a cautious walk. Fargo halted and cradled the Henry. He was hot and footsore and in no mood to put up with any nonsense.

Outlaws and cutthroats of every stripe were common in that region. Where there was no law, the lawless always thrived. Many a pilgrim had found out the hard way that the only surefire justice to be had west of the Mississippi was dispensed at the business end of a gun.

As the rider came close enough to note details, Fargo's curiosity increased. The sombrero crowned a thatch of unruly black hair, which in turn framed handsome features animated by gray eyes that danced with devilish glee. A short gray jacket and gray pants flared at the bottom were caked with dust, as was a frilly white shirt and black boots inlaid with silver stripes down the sides.

The sombrero, the clothes, a gunbelt decorated with silver studs, they were all Mexican. But the face was a mix of Spanish and white, the eyebrows thin, the mustache bushy. A hawkish nose and flawless white teeth completed the portrait. "*Hola, señor,*" the man called out. "*Hace calor hoy, eh?*"

"*Habla* English?" Fargo responded. He spoke Spanish quite well, but sometimes it paid not to let on that he did.

"*Sí señor,*" the man answered, reining up. "I speak your language." Under his breath, but loud enough for Fargo to overhear, he muttered in Spanish, "Better than you speak mine, fool. How typical." Resorting to English again, he said amiably, "It is a hot day, is it not? Much too hot for an *hombre* to be afoot in the middle of nowhere, eh?"

Fargo got right to the point. "You're following me. Why?"

"Me, *señor*? Why would I do such a thing?" Chuckling, the rider removed the sombrero and squinted at the infernal orb above them. "Especially on a day like today. Why, it is not fit for Gila monsters, let alone men."

With the hat off, the man's age was more apparent. Initially, Fargo had pegged it as twenty-five to thirty. Now, he guessed it to be around twenty, and that was probably still too generous. "Why?" he repeated harshly.

The rider in gray replaced the sombrero, then lifted the sorrel's reins. "I resent your tone, *señor*. If not for the help you gave the Howards, I would take offense. And few dare trifle with the Durango Kid."

Fargo suppressed a grin. The younger man was as brazen as a bull, and as thick-headed. He wasn't impressed by the fancy title. It had become the custom of late for any short-horn who could afford an ivory-handled pistol to give himself a colorful handle and go strutting around like a bantam rooster. "The Howards? Lucas and Clarice, you mean?"

The Durango Kid nodded. "Friends of mine, *señor*. Very close friends. I would hate to see anything happen to them."

"How is it that you just happened to be at that canyon at the same time they were?" Fargo asked.

"Would you believe it was a . . . how do you say it? . . . a coincidence?" the Durango Kid said in sham innocence.

"No."

The younger man snickered. "Neither would I, were I in your boots. But since I am in *my* boots, and what I do is none of your business, it is not anything I care to talk about. I will be on my way."

Fargo had no cause to keep the Kid there. But the water skin that hung from the sorrel's saddle reminded him of his raw throat. He moved closer. "Not so fast. I'd be obliged for a drink."

"Ah, I would imagine so. This heat. It is hotter than an

oven, is it not?" The Kid unfastened the skin, opened it, and tilted it to his mouth. Water trickled from the ends of his mouth as he drank greedily. Lowering it, he said, "I suppose I could spare a few mouthfuls. How much are they worth to you, gringo? Ten dollars? Twenty?"

"Go to hell."

The Durango Kid capped the skin. "Suit yourself, *señor*. But there are no springs anywhere around. And it is a long walk to the nearest stream." He paused, smirking. "I should think that ten dollars is very fair."

Fargo was rankled by the Kid's gall, but he did not let on. Fishing in a pocket, he pulled out a handful of coins and a few bills. "There must be thirty dollars. It's more than enough."

"*Sí*. For that much, you can drink until you burst." Chortling, the Kid leaned down to take the money. Suddenly, he found himself staring down the barrel of the Henry. His boyish countenance clouded, and he froze. "What is this, *señor?* I offer you some refreshment, and you would kill me?"

"Take it," Fargo commanded. The coins tinkled as they fell into the Kid's open palms. Fargo handed over the bills, took the water skin, and stepped well back. "All right. You wanted to be on your way. So light a shuck."

The Durango Kid glanced from the money to the skin and back again. A laugh spilled from him. "You misunderstand, *señor*. I offered you a drink. That is all. After you are done, I want the rest of my water back."

"No, you're the one who has it wrong," Fargo said evenly. "The thirty dollars if for all of it."

"Think carefully, gringo," the Kid warned. "I am not about to let you make a jackass of me. We will call this a little joke on your part, and let it go at that, eh?" He jingled the coins. "And to show you that I am not the *bastardo* you seem to think, I will give the money back and you can have a drink for free. How would that be, *señor?*"

Fargo was amused by the Kid's change of heart. It rang as true as a cracked bell. "The whole skin. Take your blood money and go." He motioned eastward. "If you hurry, you can reach one of the creeks that feed into the Animas in a couple of hours."

"You are making a mistake, *señor*. Ask anyone. I have shot down more men than you have fingers and toes for doing much less than you propose to do." The Kid's voice lowered. "Give me back my water skin, now, and we will part in peace."

"Look me up in Animas City in a couple of days if you still want it back," Fargo said. "For thirty dollars, it'll be yours."

The Kid stared hard at the Henry. Flushed with anger, he began to turn the sorrel. Fargo covered him every moment. He saw the Kid reach up as if to adjust the sombrero. Without warning the sombrero was in the Kid's hand, sweeping at his face. He batted it aside and raised the rifle again, only to be pelted by the coins. They blinded him for an instant. It was more than enough. The Durango Kid slammed into him, and they crashed to the ground.

2

Why the Durango Kid did not use his pistol, Skye Fargo had no idea. He was simply glad the man in gray was either too mad to think straight, or just plain careless. Blinded as he was, the Kid could have shot him down with no problem. But now, even as he landed on his back with the Kid astride him, Fargo swept the Henry's stock up and around. It clipped the Durango Kid on the temple and knocked him off. Surging erect, Fargo pivoted as the Kid did likewise and came at him with cocked fists.

Fargo lowered the Henry to the ground and met the *pistolero* head-on. They traded a flurry of blows. Fargo was bigger and broader at the shoulders, and his frame was packed with twice as much solid sinew. His punches staggered the Kid, tottered him backward. To his credit, though, the Durango Kid absorbed punches that would have dropped most others, and waded back into Fargo with renewed vengeance. Fargo blocked a wide looping swing from the left, delivered an uppercut, tipped a jab, and followed through with a roundhouse right that brought the Kid crashing down like a felled redwood. Standing over him, Fargo braced for another attack. To his surprise, the Durango Kid smirked and rubbed his jaw.

"*Madre de Dios!* You can hit, *amigo*. I would like to see you go up against Bruto. Now there would be fight! And I would bet on you, *señor*. Why, at the odds El Gato is likely to offer, I could win a small fortune." The Kid extended an arm. "Help me up, friend. My legs feel like they are made of that water you crave so much."

Fargo did not know what to make of this self-professed

killer. A minute ago the man had been ready to tear him apart. Now the Durango Kid was acting as if they were the best of pards. Suspicious of a trick, he said, "Not so fast. What about that water, *amigo?* Do I get to keep it without any more fuss?"

The Durango Kid pursed his lips, then chuckled. "*Sí*, with my compliments. And you may keep your money, as well. A rich man like me, I already have more *dinero* than I know what to do with."

"Is that a fact?" Fargo responded, thinking that it was his day for running into half-crazed characters. First the old mountain man, now this strange gunman. "If you have so much, why didn't you offer me a drink for free?"

"It was the principle of the thing, *amigo.* If I had given you water outright, you would think the Durango Kid was green behind the ears, as you *gringos* like to say. And I could not have that, now could I?"

In a twisted sort of way, the Kid's logic almost made sense. Still wary, Fargo gripped the offered hand and pulled the Kid up. "You'd better learn to rein in that temper of yours. Or one of these days, you'll wind up in more hot water than you can handle."

More mirth gushed from the Kid. "If you only knew, my friend. I have been in hot water since I was old enough to wear pants. I was never good enough for my parents, never bad enough for those I liked to ride with. So now I am on my own. A lone wolf, eh? And I would not have it otherwise." He moved to the sorrel, swung up, and smiled wistfully. "Life is strange, is it not? At sunrise we did not know each other, now we will be *compañeros* for life."

"I wouldn't go that far . . ." Fargo began. But the Kid was not listening. With a whoop and a wave of the sombrero, the Durango Kid trotted to the northeast. And that was that. Fargo retrieved the Henry, his money, and the water skin. Taking a long drink, he slung the clammy bag over his left shoulder and resumed his interrupted trek, feeling marvelously refreshed.

The chain of events puzzled him. A lovely woman and her cantankerous grandfather wandering the wasteland in the miserable heat. A cocky *pistolero* with more brass than brains, who just happened to be in the same area at the same time. If it was a coincidence, then Fargo was the Queen of England. He dismissed it from his mind with a shrug. Whatever they were up to was their business. All he cared about was reclaiming the Ovaro and being on his way to Texas. He had an appointment with a man in San Antonio in another week, a meeting with a distraught father who yearned to find his missing son, believed taken by the Comanches.

The minutes dragged into hours. The afternoon waxed, then waned. Fargo drank liberally to ward off the heat. His shadow had stretched into the proportions of a Goliath when he spied a thin line of pale cottonwoods and wavy willows to the east. It was too soon to be the Animas River, so it must be a feeder creek. Soon he confirmed his hunch. In the shade of a willow he set down the skin and the Henry and stripped off his boots and socks. Feet bare, he rolled up his pants and waded in. The water rose as high as his knees. He splashed some on his neck, trickled some down his chest. Soaking his red bandanna, he applied it to his face.

The crack of a twig sent a tingle down his spine. In his eagerness to cool off, he had made the cardinal mistake any frontiersman could. He had neglected to keep an eye on his surroundings. Pretending he had not heard, he slowly lowered the bandanna so he could peek out.

Someone was behind a tree on the other side of the creek. He glimpsed an elbow clad in blue fabric a split second before it disappeared. Squatting at the water's edge, he folded the bandanna and tied it around his neck. Out of the corner of an eye, he watched the tree. Part of a face poked out past the trunk for a few moments. He saw little more than the brim of a hat and a suggestion of sandy hair, then it was gone. No gun was evident. But Fargo figured that if the person was friendly, whoever it was would come right out in the open and greet him—not skulk around like a bushwhacker.

The creek narrowed farther down to a width of five feet. At that point a gravel bar projected halfway into it. Rising,

Fargo moseyed along the bank. He stared at the sky, at sparrows frolicking in a bush, at a solitary butterfly hovering over a flower, but never directly at the tree concealing the skulker. Ambling onto the gravel bar, he bent as if to examine something in the water. His right hand casually rested on the smooth butt of his Colt. From under his brows he saw a hint of blue behind the willow. The skulker was still there.

Uncoiling, Fargo exploded into motion. He cleared the creek in a single bound and bore down on the tree. The Colt streaked clear of his holster. His ruse worked, in that he caught whoever it was flatfooted. A low cry of alarm signaled the flight of a slim man in a baggy blue shirt, baggy black pants, and a floppy brown hat. It startled Fargo to discover that the man did not have a gunbelt on, nor did Fargo see a knife sheath. For someone to go around unarmed in that foreboding country was to invite trouble.

The man ran in a peculiar fashion, hips swaying wide from side to side. He glanced back once. The floppy hat covered the upper half of his face, so all that was visible was a smooth chin and his cheeks. Facing front, he ran faster. Ahead were two cottonwoods spaced close together. There was barely enough room between them for a cat to squeeze through, but the man in the floppy hat never slowed down or changed course. Turning sideways, he tried to barrel on through, only to be brought up short when his shoulders and hips became wedged fast. Small hands pushed at one of the trees in futile effort.

By then, Fargo had put two and two together. Grabbing the skulker's wrist, he yanked so hard that the person was not only pulled free, but tumbled to the ground. The floppy hat fell. From under it spilled luxurious raven tresses. Green eyes narrowed in anger. The woman's shirt was unbuttoned at the top, and it shifted, revealing a creamy taste of upper breast. "How dare you lay a hand on me! Who do you think you are? When the men at Animas City hear about this, they'll make you the guest of honor at a necktie social."

While it was true that abusing a woman in the West

25

brought swift retribution, Fargo had to laugh at the notion that he would be hanged for what he had just done. It made her madder, and she came up off the ground, spoiling for a fight.

"Think I'm funny, do you, stranger?" She balled her fists and shook them in his face. "If I were a man, I'd beat you silly."

Fargo believed she was tempted to try anyway. He had stumbled on a regular wildcat, complete with long nails, which she raked at an eye. Only his lightning reflexes spared him. Seizing her wrist, he held it locked in his grip while she tugged and twisted and hissed like a viper. "Calm down, lady. No harm has been done, other than to your pride. And that wouldn't have happened if you weren't sneaking around like a fool kid playing hide-and-seek."

It was not his day for saying the right thing. She sputtered like a geyser about to blow, then aimed a kick at his shin that he nimbly avoided. "Are you saying I'm a *child?*"

"If the boot fits," Fargo quipped, and had to dodge two more kicks, one propelled a lot higher up. Suddenly spinning her by the arm, he stuck out a foot and tripped her. She vented an unladylike squawk as she was dumped onto her backside. "Sit there and calm down. I'm not out to do you any harm."

"Which is more than *I* can say." With that, she rammed both feet into Fargo's legs. They were swept out from under him and down he went, onto his posterior in front of her. The look on his face must have been comical because the raven-haired beauty laughed lustily, her moods as mercurial as the weather. "Serves you right, mister! I hope you broke your butt."

Fargo could not help but share her merriment. When she stopped and cast a nervous look at the Colt, he holstered the pistol and held out his hand. "Let's start over." He told her his name. "Sorry about the little misunderstanding. I don't make a habit out of manhandling women."

"Wanda Howard," she said, scrutinizing his features and the set of his broad shoulders. Her nose was upturned at the tip, lending her an impish quality that had not been apparent when she was as mad as a wet hen. "I reckon I know better than to spy on folks, but I wasn't sure if you were friendly or not. A lot of bad men roam these parts."

"Did you say Howard?" Fargo asked. "Any relation to Lucas and Clarice?"

Wanda's lower jaw dropped. "My grandpa and my younger sister! You know them?"

Briefly, Fargo recounted his encounter, ending with, "So I'm headed for Animas City to get my horse back. How far do I have to go yet?"

"Not more than an hour if you ride double with me," Wanda proposed. "It's the least I can do after you helped Gramps and Sis." She scanned the wasteland to the west. "You must be made of iron if you came across that oven."

Standing, Fargo helped her up. "It wasn't as bad as it could have been. A *compañero* of mine called the Durango Kid gave me a water skin."

It was an idle comment, half in jest. Yet it had a remarkable effect on Wanda Howard. She uttered a tiny growl and gnashed her teeth. "I knew it! I just knew it!"

"Knew what?"

"Nothing. It's a family matter," Wanda said, and rotated. "I'll fetch my horse and be right back."

The sway to her hips, Fargo observed, was as obvious when she walked as when she ran. The woman was pure female, and no amount of baggy clothes could hide the fact. He wondered what she was doing there by her lonesome, and why she saw fit to disguise who she was. And why had she grown so upset at the mention of the Durango Kid? Had she come to meet him? Were they lovers?

Too many questions and not enough answers, Fargo mused. Recrossing the creek, he shouldered the water skin. Wanda emerged from the bush, mounted on a fine zebra dun. A rifle jutted from the boot.

"I hope you won't mind riding double with me."

She had to be kidding. Fargo draped the water skin over the saddle horn, gripped the cantle, and forked leather, nestling snug behind her. Up close, her hair had a minty scent, and her body gave off arousing warmth. To be polite, he placed his hands on the edge of the cantle. "Ready when you are."

"You'd better hold onto me," Wanda suggested. "I mean to reach Animas City in a hurry."

Fargo was not about to argue. Looping both arms around her waist, he felt the baggy shirt yield to the pressure until his arms were firm around her compact form. She was as nicely built as her younger sister. To judge by how her shirt swelled at the top, she was even more amply endowed. Her muscular thighs gripped the dun with little bounce to them, sign of a skilled rider. At a brisk walk she left the belt of vegetation and bore to the northeast, bringing her mount to a trot. She twisted to speak, and for a stimulating instant their mouths almost touched. Catching herself, she shifted forward a smidgen.

"So tell me. How long have you known the Durango Kid?"

"We met for the first time today," Fargo revealed.

"But I thought you said that he's your *compañero?* Your partner?"

"His words, not mine. Other than he likes to hear himself talk, and probably is partial to admiring his reflection in the mirror, I couldn't tell you a thing about him."

"I can," Wanda declared. "He's a no-account gunman. A *pistolero*, he styles himself. Struts around with that expensive Colt of his like he owns the world. Word is he's shot down over a dozen men. Vile, despicable, mean, his whole lot. This country would be better off if we were rid of every last desperado."

"The Durango Kid is no badman," Fargo said flatly. For all the Kid's bluster, the Kid wasn't a typical coldhearted killer, or he would have gunned Fargo down when he had the opportunity.

"How can you say that? By your own admittance, you hardly know him." Wanda sniffed as if she had detected a foul odor. "Trust me. The Durango Kid will come to grief before too long. And cause a lot, in turn, for those who care for him." Fargo could feel her tense in his arms. "I wish to high heaven someone had gunned him down long ago."

Did she care for the Kid? Was that why she was so disturbed? Since she was being so talkative, Fargo probed further. "What can you tell me about his background?"

"Plenty. His real name is Alonzo de Leon. He's the son of a wealthy landowner whose family was here before any whites arrived. They were given a land grant by the Mexican government of over four thousand acres and stayed on after the war."

The war she referred to was the clash with Mexico in 1846. The United States won, and as part of a treaty signed afterward, the U.S. government agreed to honor all prewar grants issued by the Mexican government to settlers in the remote northern reaches of Mexico's frontier, land that was now part and parcel of the Colorado Territory. Some whites resented that the Mexican landowners had prior claim to some of the very best land to be found in the whole region.

Wanda continued. "Alonzo de Leon was raised in the lap of luxury. His father, Manuel, groomed him to take over after he dies, but Alonzo wanted nothing to do with *hacienda* life. It was too dull, too boring for him. So he wandered off to Mexico for a year or so, and when he came back, he was packing that fancy Colt and calling himself the Durango Kid." She paused. "The story goes that he was in a number of shootouts down in Durango, Mexico. That's where he picked up the new handle."

"You seem to know an awful lot about the de Leon family," Fargo mentioned.

"People love to gossip about the rich and powerful, Mr. Fargo. And the de Leons are the most influential family in these parts. It's only natural that whatever they do would be fodder for the gossip mill."

"I suppose."

They rode in silence for a while, broken only by the thud of hooves and the heavy breathing of the zebra dun. The double weight was beginning to tell when Wanda slowed to a walk. She fidgeted often, restless, anxious to reach their destination. Fargo prompted her to talk again by asking, "Animas City must have sprung up overnight. It wasn't here the last time I passed through."

"It's a quaint community," Wanda said. "Came at just the right time, too. Before, the farmers and ranchers had to travel clear to Denver for supplies, which took weeks in the winter. And then only if the high passes were open. Half the time there was too much snow for a team to get over the Divide."

"Is there a lawman?"

Wanda shook her head, her hair swirling about her shoulders and brushing against Fargo's face, tickling him. "I wish. We could use one. Hardcases like El Gato have made our lives miserable."

"The Cat," Fargo translated. "The Durango Kid mentioned him. Who is he?"

"The worst mother's-son who ever donned britches," Wanda said. "He robbed and plundered down in Mexico until the *federales* made it too hot for him to operate. To escape, he strayed north of the border with a dozen vile vermin. He has a sanctuary somewhere up in the mountains and comes down from time to time to raid and kill. Last autumn he wiped out a family on Elk Creek. Murdered the father and two sons, raped the mother and a fourteen-year-old girl. Took everything they had."

"Is the Kid part of El Gato's bunch?"

"Not that I've heard tell," Wanda answered. "Rumor has it that they're not on the best of terms. It would be wonderful if they threw down on each other and killed each other off. Two birds with one stone, so to speak."

Fargo gazed thoughtfully at the La Plata mountains, then in the direction of the more distant San Juans. "Why don't the farmers and ranchers band together and hunt El Gato down? Or call in the army?"

"Our mayor led a delegation to Denver. Guess what a general there told him? The army has its hands full with the Southern insurrection. Troops can't be spared to cope with our 'little' problem. Not when we're so far off the beaten path." Wanda's tone left no doubt as to what she would like to do to the military authorities. "As for hunting the bandit down ourselves, don't think we wouldn't if we could. But our menfolk are farmers and cattle herders. Few of them can track worth a hoot. And most of those are married."

"What does that have to do with anything?"

Wanda snickered. "Spoken like a gent who has never tied the knot. Mister, nine times out of ten, it's the women who rule the roost. None of the wives hereabouts favor the idea of having their husbands brought home belly-down over a horse."

Fargo could not believe the settlers would rather be picked off one by one instead of mounting a campaign to wipe out the The Cat and his ilk. "Surely there must be someone—" he began.

"Oh, a few men tried to do something. Two farmers, Elmer and Jeffrey, volunteered. Since they were once buffalo hunters, they figured that they had a fair-to-middling chance. Took their old Sharps rifles and a mule and enough grub to last a month." Wanda swiveled. "They were never seen again." She ran a hand through her hair. "Then there was the jasper our mayor imported from Denver. He claimed to be a gunman. Owned a pair of shiny Remingtons and a scattergun. Our mayor paid him half his fee in advance, and off he went, into the San Juans. No one ever saw him again, either. Some think he pocketed the money and skipped. Personally, I reckon his bleached bones are lying up on a high slope somewhere for the marmots and chipmunks to gnaw on."

Animas City was literally caught between a rock and a hard place. Unless the people rallied or hired a professional assassin, El Gato's depredations would go on and on. Once news filtered back East, newcomers would shun the settlement. Eventually, it would die off, devastating the homesteaders. As soon as pickings were slim, The Cat would pack up and move elsewhere—to start the whole savage cycle over again.

Wanda was speaking. "Maybe you'd like to give it a try, Fargo. You would earn a thousand dollars if you brought in El Gato's head."

"That's a lot of money," Fargo admitted—more than most respectable citizens earned in half a year. He thought of the wild times he could have, the poker games and nights spent with bawdy women.

"Everyone pitched in and contributed a share. The biggest chunk came from a surprising source. Five hundred, courtesy of Manuel de Leon." Wanda clucked to the dun. "De Leon hates El Gato. You could say rubbing The Cat out has become an obsession with him. From time to time he ventures into the high country with his *vaqueros*, but so far they've come up empty-handed."

"Has El Gato ever struck at the *hacienda?*"

"On five or six occasions. Manuel has lost scores of cattle and a few good hands. He's vowed publicly to plant The Cat, if it's the last thing he ever does."

From then on they made small talk. Fargo learned that Lucas Howard had indeed been a free trapper in the old days. When Norman, his son, came to the region ten years ago, Lucas had made himself to home and never left. Five years past, a flood had claimed Norman and his wife. Lucas promptly appointed himself protector and guardian of the sisters.

"Not that we need any watching over," Wanda said. "We're big girls. We can take care of ourselves." She qualified her statement. "Most of the time, anyhow."

The transition between the near-desert realm and the web of verdant valleys fed by runoff from the snow-packed summits was striking. One moment Fargo and Wanda were climbing a rocky slope, the land around them parched and stark. The next, they were on the crown, and in front of them unfolded green fields dotted by stands of tall trees. Scattered homesteads were bordered by neatly tilled fields. Cows grazed at random. To the southeast a man and his son tilled the soil.

Wanda smiled and said, "Isn't it beautiful? We've made a paradise of the wilderness. One day, farms and towns will stretch clear from the Atlantic Ocean to the Pacific. It's our Manifest Destiny. Even the president says so."

Fargo did not share the common opinion. Yes, those in government believed that America had a divine right to push her borders from shore to shore. Yes, the newspapers had been harping on the Destiny business for quite some time. But where Wanda approved of the relentless press of civilization, Fargo did not. Little by little, the wild places were being chipped away. Parcel by parcel, the wilderness was being turned into farmland. Towns sprouted where pristine forest once reigned. The plains were being slowly but inevitably eaten away from east to west, as if by a cancer.

Where would it all end? Fargo had often asked himself. Only when towns and cities occupied every available plot? When America was knee-deep in people? When the virgin land Fargo loved so well was completely gone? Should that happen, the freedom to roam as he pleased would be gone with it.

Wanda guided the zebra dun to a rutted road that wound northward. "Another couple of miles and we'll be there," she announced.

A golden halo crowned the horizon. Soon the sun relinquished the heavens to the first of the twinkling stars, and twilight descended. The weary dun plodded along. Wanda stifled yawns. To the northwest towered Hesperus Mountain, ridges radiating from the crest like the spokes of a gigantic wheel. Those ridges formed forested ramparts that separated the lush valleys in which many of the settlers had taken root. The tinkle of cowbells blended with the moan of the wind gusting from higher elevations.

"How long will you be staying in Animas City?" Wanda unexpectedly asked.

"I haven't made up my mind yet," Fargo said.

"You're welcome to stay with my sister and me. We have a room to spare."

"What would Lucas say?"

The clatter of hooves cut off her reply. Down a narrow trail on the right galloped a trio of burly horsemen attired in overalls and homespun shirts. Farmers, Fargo guessed. In the forefront was a solid oak of a man whose square jaw was twice as wide as his forehead. "Wanda!" he hollered. "Hold up!"

"Oh, no," Wanda said, reluctantly drawing rein. To

Fargo she said urgently, "Just sit tight and let me do the talking. We don't want any trouble."

At a comment from the human oak, the trio fanned out, one man moving in front of the dun, another behind it. The oak halted broadside to Wanda's animal and cast a cold appraisal at Fargo. "What's going on here, gal? Didn't I tell you that I won't abide you foolin' around with other fellers?"

"Now, just you sheath your claws, Harve Porter," Wanda snapped. "How many times must I tell you that I'm not your woman, and never will be? I can ride with anyone I please."

"Reckon so, do you?" Harve Porter said, nudging his horse closer. "Well, you're wrong." His left arm shot out and fingers as thick as railroad spikes clamped onto Fargo's buckskin shirt. "I'll prove it by bustin' this buzzard's head clean open."

3

Skye Fargo was sick and tired of being treated as a whipping boy. Lucas Howard had nearly torn into him, the Durango Kid had tried to punch his face in, and now a farmer he had never met, someone he had never wronged in any way, was about to cave in his skull over a simple misunderstanding. It was too much. Inside, something snapped. Even as Harve Porter went to haul him from the zebra dun, Fargo brought the Henry's stock up and around and smashed it flush against Porter's noggin. The human oak blinked once, grunted, and keeled over, thudding to the ground headfirst.

Immediately, Harve's friends closed in, one from the left, one from the right. The only guns they had were rifles that hung from their saddle horns with the barrels held in place by latches under their legs. Since neither man made any attempt to grab one and open fire, Fargo did not shoot them down as they converged. Quickly reversing his grip on the Henry, he swung it in a high arc to avoid accidentally hitting Wanda. The farmer on the right threw up both arms, but the force of the blow toppled him. The second man tried to duck, but he was a shade too slow. The stock clipped the top of his head, and a moment later he was lying prone, hands clasped to his bloody scalp, howling loud enough to rival a wolf.

Harve Porter did not stay down long. Growling like the grizzly Fargo had tangled with earlier, Porter shoved to his feet and made as if to lunge at Fargo. The rasp of the Henry's lever stopped him cold.

"Not another step," Fargo said through gritted teeth.

Wanda, overcome by mute horror, regained the use of

her vocal chords. "Enough, Harve! Try that again, and I swear that I'll never speak to you for as long as I live!"

It was not much of a threat, in Fargo's opinion, but it served to give Porter second thoughts. The big farmer scowled and clenched his ham-sized fists. "I ain't never been whipped before, gal. It don't sit right with me."

Fargo had the front sight centered on Porter's forehead. "There's a first time for everything, mister," he said. "Be thankful you're still breathing."

Porter glared, unfazed. "We'll meet again. And the next time it will be different." He leaned forward and raised both huge fists for emphasis. "The next time, I'm going to pound you into the dirt."

"*Men!*" Wanda declared, and applied her heels to the dun. As they trotted off, Harve Porter's bellow followed them.

"I'll see you in Animas City, mister! Be ready! When you least expect, I'll step out of the shadows and wallop the stuffing out of you! Just see if I don't!"

There was more, but Fargo refused to listen. To Wanda, he said, "What was that all about?" As if he could not guess.

"Harve has been partial to me for a good long while. He's told everyone and anyone that we're to be married one of these days. But if I've made it plain once, I've made it plain a thousand times that I'd as soon marry a Comanche. Harve just can't seem to take the hint." She tilted her head around. "I must say, I've never seen anyone handle him and his cousins as smoothly as you did. Why, compared to you, they were moving in slow motion. You're a hellion when you get your dander up." In a throaty purr, she concluded, "I like that in a man."

Another time, another place, and Fargo would have taken that as his cue to gauge exactly how much she liked it. But after the day he'd had, his sole interest was in locating the Ovaro, treating himself to a room at a hotel, and soaking in a tub for an hour. Afterward, well, who could say?

Another couple of miles brought them into a wide valley. Sprinkled here and there were the lights of farmhouses. In the center flourished a cluster of oversized fireflies that burned brightly in the darkening night.

"Animas City," Wanda stated happily.

As Fargo shortly learned, calling it a "city" was stretching the truth a mite. A single dirt street was flanked by five buildings to the west, seven to the east. In addition to two saloons, it boasted a livery, a general store, a feed supply and farm implement mercantile, a land office, and sundry establishments found in practically every settlement on the frontier. One type, though, was conspicuous by its absence.

"There's no hotel," Fargo commented as the zebra dun plodded down the middle of the street.

Wanda chortled. "Animas City isn't Denver. Give us another five to ten years and we'll have one every bit as grand as the Imperial." She pointed at cabins and a few frame homes to the north. "Besides, what do you need a hotel for? You're staying with us, remember? I won't take no for an answer."

From a saloon they were passing gusted course laughter and the tinny tinkle of a piano. To Fargo's surprise, Wanda reined toward it and stopped at a hitching post that barely had room for one more horse. "Come here often?"

"Be sensible," Wanda retorted, and pointed at a flight of stairs to the left of the building. Nailed to the wall next to them was a small sign. Thanks to light spilling from a window, Fargo could read it. "Dr. Henry Carver, M.D.," he said aloud.

"Doc Carver is the only sawbones for a hundred miles around," Wanda said. "We're lucky to have him. Back when Animas City first sprang up, he only came by once every two months on his regular circuits. Then he took a shine to the widow Tucker. Lo and behold, the next we knew, he had set up permanent practice here."

Fargo slid down and stretched his stiff legs. He held up a hand to help Wanda, but she dismounted on her own, looped the reins around the hitching post, and headed for the stairs. "If Lucas was as bad off as you seemed to think, then this is where he will be. Come along if you want."

The Ovaro was not one of the animals present. In order

to find out where the stallion was, Fargo tagged along. At Wanda's knock, the door was opened by a portly man in a white shirt with rolled-up sleeves and scarlet stains. Spectacles perched on the rim of his nose. "Wanda, my dear!" the physician exclaimed. "At last! Clarice went to fetch you shortly after she brought your grandfather in, but you were nowhere to be found. She's beside herself with worry. Where have you been?"

"I went to visit a friend," Wanda lied.

Doc Carver admitted them and closed the door. Giving Fargo close scrutiny, he said, "That's a nice new Henry repeater you've got there, mister. Not many Henrys in these parts. You wouldn't happen to be the man who helped drive off that grizzly, would you? Clarice mentioned that the man who did owned a rifle just like yours."

"I was there, but the real credit should go to the Durango Kid," Fargo said.

The sawbones blinked. "You don't say. How curious. Interesting that Clarice never saw fit to mention his part in the affair." Carver began to roll down his right sleeve. "In any event, old Lucas is fortunate to be alive. When he was first brought in, I feared his lung had been punctured. But now I'm satisfied that he only has two broken ribs. Which is enough to keep him bedridden for a week or better."

"Can we see him?" Wanda inquired, glancing at a partially open door to the left of the foyer.

"Only if you promise not to tire him. He's awake, but as weak as a newborn kitten."

Wanda hurried to the door. Fargo figured that she would want to be alone with the old man, but she beckoned. A single bed dominated the comfortably furnished room. As pale as the sheet on which he lay was Lucas Howard, his head propped on a pair of pillows. A wan smile curled his mouth, and he croaked, "Wanda, girl! Where in tarnation have you been! I was worried sick. Even sent a rider to have the Porter clan come in so we could organize a search in the morning."

"So that's why Harve was on his way into town," Wanda said. Sitting on the edge of the bed, she tenderly clasped her grandfather's weathered hand. "I'm sorry. I didn't mean to upset you. I went for a long ride, is all."

Lucas's gaze drifted to Fargo. "You again!" he declared. "Clarice told me what you did. How you lent her your pinto, and everything. I reckon I owe you my life." He tried to sit up, but broke into a coughing fit. Wanda gently eased him back down. "You sure have a knack for showing up at the oddest places, friend. How'd you get here so soon? Did you find Jezebel?"

Fargo wished that he could say he had. The mountain man was quite attached to that feisty bay. "Wanda brought me in."

"Do tell," Lucas said, bestowing a quizzical expression on his granddaughter. "When you said you went on a long ride, girl, I had no idea just *how* long. I think you've got a heap of explaining to do."

"I'd like to know where my stallion is," Fargo mentioned before they got into it.

"At the livery," Lucas said. "That animal of yours is something else, friend. Has more sand than most ten critters. Clarice held it to a trot for miles on end, and it never gave out." More coughing afflicted him. Covering his mouth, he said between his fingers, "We told George, the livery owner, to take real good care of it. Oats and hay and the whole works."

Nodding, Fargo stepped to the doorway, pausing when Wanda said his name.

"Don't forget where you're staying tonight. I'll swing by the livery to pick you up on my way out."

Lucas puffed out his cheeks. "What the devil? Do you want to be the talk of the town? Having a man under the same roof as two single girls? What will folks think?"

"Frankly, grandpa, I don't give a damn."

Fargo left. Doc Carver hustled by to nip the spat in the bud and gave him a kindly wink. Once outside, Fargo hurried down the street to the stable. Animas City was quiet except for the noise issuing from the saloons. Somewhere off in the farmland a coyote yipped. A dog in town answered.

The wide double doors were closed. Fargo pried one open and went in. A single lantern illuminated the interior. Half the stalls were empty. Straw littered the center aisle, along with droppings the owner had been too lazy to shovel up. "Anyone here?" he called out. Receiving no reply, he inspected each stall until he came to the one containing the Ovaro. The stallion had been dozing. Scenting him, it snorted and bobbed its head in greeting. Fargo stroked its neck, then examined its legs and shoes. The latter were intact, and there was no swelling. No harm had been done.

An empty bucket hung on a nearby peg. Helping himself to it, Fargo hunted for the oak bin and found it along the rear wall. Using a scoop that lay on top of the grain, he filled the bucket and treated the Ovaro. While the pinto ate, he went in search of his saddle. He found it in the tack room, along with his saddlebags and bedroll. Satisfied, he emerged and walked to the central aisle. Suddenly, shadows detached themselves from the front of the stable, barring his path.

"Remember us, you son of a bitch?"

Harve Porter and his cousins were in town. Harve held a pitchfork. On the right was a burly cousin holding a singletree, the crossbar to which the traces of a wagon's team were attached. It made a nasty club. Off to the left was the second cousin, armed with a bullwhip. All items they had picked up in the stable.

"Let it be," Fargo said.

"Not on your life, polecat," Harve said. "I told you that we'd pay you back, and here we are. Only this time we aim to do the job right. The only way you'll leave here is if you crawl out on your busted hands and knees."

"You're forgetting something," Fargo said, and brought the Henry up. But they were expecting that. The bullwhip cracked, the lash wrapping around the rifle's barrel and jerking it aside. Fargo braced himself and tried to wrench the Henry free. In rushed Harve, the pitchfork raised overhead. Fargo had to let go or be impaled. Skipping to one side, he planted a fist in Harve's gut. It was like punching a sack of potatoes. The farmer was all muscle. The blow hardly slowed him.

Bringing his fist up to hit Harve in the face, Fargo caught movement on his right. The cousin with the single-tree had charged, the crossbar hiked. Fargo backpedaled and collided with a stall. Unable to retreat any farther, he crouched, and as the single-tree swept down, he danced out of range to the left. Which put him directly in front of Harve again, who bellowed like a longhorn, extended the pitchfork, and barreled toward him.

Fargo twisted at the very last moment. The glittering tines missed his chest by a prairie dog's whisker. He grabbed the handle and pivoted, throwing his left leg out. It caught Harve across the shins, and the big farmer went down, sliding half a dozen feet into a pile of dung. Rotating, Fargo swooped a hand to his Colt. But again the bullwhip thwarted him. The stinging lash wrapped around his wrist, jerking his arm away from the pistol. Wrenching backward, he tore at the rawhide.

From out of the shadows came the cousin with the single-tree. It arched from on high. Fargo saved himself by leaping as far back as the whip would allow. The crossbar struck the taut braided leather, flaring pain up his arm to his shoulder. Right away the cousin pivoted for another swing. Fargo kicked out, the tip of his boot landing where it would hurt the most. Yelping, the cousin doubled over, the single-tree nearly falling from fingers gone momentarily limp.

The precious moments Fargo had bought were all he needed to tear the whip from his wrist. He faced the cousin holding it, only to hear the *clomp* of heavy feet to his rear. Darting to the left, he was nearly bowled over when Harve Porter's shoulder rammed into his. Harve skittered to a lurching stop, then rotated, his contorted face marred by brown smudges.

"Damn you!" the big farmer roared. "You're quicker than a jackrabbit!" Glancing at the man with the bullwhip, Harve rasped, "Keep him from dodgin' me, Otto, or I'll take that thing and shove it down your throat."

The lash streaked toward Fargo. He evaded the tip, then

dashed toward the lantern. His aim was to extinguish it and plunge the stable in total darkness. But he had taken only two strides when the rawhide looped around his lower legs, bringing him down hard. His elbows bore the brunt. Rolling over, he saw Harve Porter hurtling toward him. The tines speared at his midriff. Wrenching to the right, Fargo heard the pitchfork *thunk* into the ground. He grabbed it and held on for dear life as Harve sought to wrest it from his grasp.

"Otto! Len! We've got him now, fellers! Lend me a hand!"

Len was still doubled over, but he gamely shuffled closer. Otto obeyed Harve, too, and in doing so, put slack on the whip that had not been there before. Enough slack for Fargo to scramble backward, tuck at the waist, and rip the rawhide from his legs.

Harve grew livid. Like a man berserk, he waded down the aisle, cleaving the air with the pitchfork again and again in a wild bid to impale Fargo. Five, six, seven times he tried. On the eighth swing the tines sank into a stall, imbedding so deeply that Harve could not pull them out. Grunting, he propped both feet firmly to apply extra strength.

Only Fargo noticed that Harve had made a crucial mistake. The enraged human oak was now between him and the cousins. Otto and Len could not get at him. Not having to worry about the bullwhip, Fargo did the last thing Harve anticipated. He attacked, connecting with a solid right that jolted the farmer, then with an uppercut that lifted Harve onto the tips of his toes. A third punch, a roundhouse, sent Harve stumbling rearward into Otto and Len. Otto managed to leap into an empty stall to safety, but Len was plowed under by Harve's greater bulk.

Fargo palmed the Colt. When Otto sprang into the aisle and snapped his arm back, Fargo fired. The slug smashed into the heavy stock, which was weighted with lead. Otto cried out, his hand stung terribly, as the bullwhip went flying.

Len was on one knee. He looked up, saw the smoke curling from the end of the Colt, and dropped the single-tree as if were a hot coal. "No more, mister," he said. "It's over, as far as I'm concerned. This wasn't my notion, anyhow."

But Harve Porter was too furious to be rational. He had lost the pitchfork when he fell. Unarmed, he bounded forward, his eyes glazed like those of a rabid beast. Fargo feinted to the left, and when Harve compensated and dived at his legs, Fargo adroitly skipped beyond Harve's reach. Harve landed on his belly. Placing both huge hands flat, he began to rise. Fargo was ready. Three times he pistol-whipped the farmer across the temple. On the third blow, Harve exhaled loudly and crumpled like a piece of paper to lie still, drool dribbling over his lower lip.

Otto took a step, glowering.

Fargo pointed the six-shooter at him and thumbed back the hammer. "Don't be as stupid as this ox," he said, nudging Harve with his boot. "I've taken all I'm going to take. Next time, I shoot to kill."

Len grabbed his brother's overalls. "Enough, Otto. Let Harve get himself planted six feet under if he wants. Hell, Wanda ain't our girl. She ain't even Harve's."

Fargo wagged the Colt at the unconscious bull at his feet. "Tote him home. And convince him to stay away from me, or else."

They had to drag Porter, he was so heavy. Puffing and panting, they exited the livery. Fargo hoped that he had seen the last of them, but something warned him that Harve Porter was not the type to take sage advice. Harve would jump him again, given half the chance. If he stayed in Animas City, he must be on his guard every minute from then on.

Holstering the revolver, Fargo brushed himself off, inspected the Henry to ensure it had not been damaged, and gave the pinto a few final pats. Cautiously, he strode into the night. The farmers were nowhere to be seen. Nor had Wanda left the doctor's office. To pass the time while he waited, Fargo made a beeline to the nearest saloon. It also happened to be the loudest.

A motley assortment of farmers, ranchers, and townspeople were drinking, gambling, and just plain socializing.

Card tables covered fully half the floor. Mingling with the players and other customers were doves in colorful tight dresses. None of them paid much attention to Fargo as he threaded through the tables. On a small stage two scantily attired women danced to a tune being pounded out by a piano player who had a near-empty pitcher of beer on the seat next to his leg.

By Eastern standards, the saloon was coarse, the patrons not much better. But as the old saw went, it didn't pay to judge a book by its cover. Those who forged a living on the frontier were hardy specimens, men and women alike. They lived rough lives, relished rough pleasures. Take, for instance, a rancher who had spent the past twelve hours out on the range, dealing with stubborn cattle and the elements. A place like the Acme was a little slice of heaven on earth—an oasis where he could relax with a drink or three, dabble at cards or dice, and maybe get to pat the posterior of a prancing dove before heading home.

Fargo deposited the Henry on the counter and kept his hand on it. From where he stood, he could see the entrance clearly. No one would be able to sneak inside without being spotted. He gestured at the barkeep, but the man was busy with another customer. Then another. Continually on the go, the bartender did not have a moment's rest. Fargo forgot about him and was observing a game of five-card stud when fingers plucked at his sleeve.

"Here's your drink, stranger."

A glass of whiskey was in front of Fargo. "How did you guess?" he said, lifting it.

"I'm no wizard, if that's what you're thinking." The barkeep bobbed his double chin at the far end of the bar. "Your *compañero* said to tell you that this one is on him."

"My . . . ?" Fargo said, and turned. A knot of customers had parted to reveal a dashing young man in gray, including a gray sombrero tilted at a rakish slant. The Durango Kid smirked and raised his own glass in salute.

"It none of my business, you understand," the bartender said, leaning over, "but if he's really your friend, you'd be smart to get him out of town while you can. Rumor has it that a pair of gun-sharks already have a plot on Boot Hill staked out with his name on it."

"Does he know?"

"Of course. I warned him myself."

"Neighborly of you. I was told that most of the locals can't stand him."

"The Kid? Oh, he likes to brag on himself and show off with that ivory-handled pistol of his. But deep down he's pretty decent. 'Course, don't tell him I said that or I'll call you a liar. He sees himself as some sort of hard-as-nails killer."

"Interesting." Fargo started to move down the bar. "Would you happen to know the two gunnies on sight if you saw them?"

"Mexican *pistoleros*. They were in here earlier asking after the Kid." The bartender scratched the stubble on his chin. "My helper has a hunch they ride for El Gato, the *bandido*, and I'm inclined to agree. They're just the type who would."

Pausing, Fargo slid enough money for five drinks across the counter. "If you spot them, signal me."

The Durango Kid was downing the last of his rotgut when Fargo reached the corner. "*Buenas noches, señor*," he said cheerfully. "Did you sprout wings and fly? Or are you part Gila monster, that you can cross such rough country in a single day without the heat sapping your energy?"

"I had your water skin, remember," Fargo joked.

"How could I forget? It is the reason I am here. I figured to collect it tomorrow when you dragged into town." The Durango Kid poured himself another shot from a half-empty bottle at his elbow. "Care for more, *amigo?*"

"I haven't touched this one yet," Fargo said, then swallowed. The coffin varnish scorched his throat on a burning path to his vitals. Soothing warmth spread rapidly. "*Gracias.*"

The Durango Kid's eyes twinkled. "It was either buy you a drink or shoot you, and I am in too fine a mood to spoil it with bloodshed tonight."

"Don't hold back on my account."

The Kid's guffaws drew curious stares from nearby drinkers. "An *hombre* after my own heart! How sad that you go around stealing water and who-knows-what-else from innocent travelers like myself. One day your wicked habits will catch up with you, *señor*, and you will regret that you did not heed your *madre* when you were little, and stick to the straight and narrows, as your preachers call it."

"We have another saying. One about the kettle calling the pot black."

"Eh?"

"Cooking utensils. They're always black."

"I still do not comprehend."

"Did you listen to your mother? Or is she happy that her son wandered south of the border and acquired a reputation as someone who packs his hardware loose?" Fargo polished off the rest of his whiskey in a single gulp.

"So. You have been asking about me. I don't know whether to be flattered or offended."

"A friend of yours volunteered some of your family history." Fargo deliberately did not go on until the Kid was shifting his weight from one foot to the other. "Wanda Howard found me out in the hardrock country and brought me in."

"Wanda? But what was she doing so far from Animas City?" The Kid rested his forearms on the bar and bent his head, pondering. "Every time I run into you, *amigo*, I get a new surprise. She and I must have a serious talk very soon."

Fargo was about to ask for more whiskey when he saw the bartender point at him, then at the entrance. Into the saloon stalked a pair of swarthy men in dark clothes similar to the Kid's, their sombreros low over their bushy brows. One was lean and wiry, the other stocky and sweaty. Both wore two guns, tied low. They stopped to give the room a predatory survey. Almost by magic, the voices fell to a subdued mutter. The piano player stroked the keys lightly instead of pounding them, and the dancers slowed to an outlandish crawl. A palpable atmosphere of fear spread among the patrons. Wolves were in the den.

The tall *pistolero* spotted the Durango Kid and nudged his companion. Side by side they crossed toward their prey, the customers parting to give them plenty of space. Halting six feet off, they focused solely on the Kid, who ignored them. "You there. Half-breed. Put down that glass and pay attention to your betters," the tall gunman declared.

When the Kid took a sip without replying, the stocky *pistolero* snickered. "He is afraid, Ramon. This spawn of Manuel de Leon and a St. Louis whore is wetting his pants, scared to face us."

The saloon fell completely silent, a collective breath held. The Durango Kid turned.

4

Skye Fargo had to hand it to the Durango Kid. Most men would have quaked in their boots on being confronted by two hardcases like Ramon and his stocky friend. But Alonzo de Leon stood there calmly and coolly and smiled at the pair of killers. His right arm slowly lowered to his side, movement the gun-sharks were keen to note. In Spanish, he said, "Good evening, gentlemen. Am I to take it that this is personal? You have a grudge against me of which I am unaware?"

The stocky *pistolero* snorted and replied in the same language. "Does a man need an excuse to squash a bug? Whether it is personal or not is unimportant. What matters is that in a short while you will be lying on the floor with your blood pumping form a dozen holes. And we will each be five thousand dollars richer."

"Ah. Then it is not personal," the Durango Kid said. "Someone is paying you the princely sum of ten thousand dollars to kill me." He paused. "Dollars, not pesos, eh? Now who do I know who has that much American money and also hates me enough to pay to have me gunned down?"

"His name is of no consequence," the stocky killer said.

Ramon glanced sharply at his partner. "Enough chatter, Lopez. Let us get this over with and ride out before these *gringos* take it into their heads to interfere."

"One moment, if you please," the Durango Kid said suavely. "At least satisfy my curiosity. Tell me who hired you."

"Maybe it was your mother," Lopez sneered.

The Kid's smile evaporated. "That is twice you have insulted her. Yet how is it that two men I have never met know she is an Americano? How is it that you know I have a soft spot in my heart for her? And that anyone who insults her winds up dead?"

"Brave words, brat," Ramon said.

"We know all about your family," Lopez boasted. "Our employer told us how your father went on a business trip to St. Louis, met the daughter of an acquaintance, and fell so madly in love that he married her six months later. An American! When he could have taken his pick of any Mexican woman he wanted!"

"You hate *gringos*, I gather?" the Kid said while shifting slightly.

"They are pigs. They always look down their noses at us, as if we are scum. This is what I would do to all of them if I could." Lopez spat at his feet and stomped on the spit with a boot heel.

"I will admit that they can grate on the nerves," the Durango Kid said. "But some of them are kind and decent. My mother, for instance. Never was a gentler soul born. Travelers who stop at our *hacienda* are always well fed and given soft beds in which to rest. She donates large sums each year to the church, for the poor. She supports an orphanage for orphans of mixed descent in Sonora. An angel, my mother."

Fargo saw that Ramon was growing impatient. He wondered if the Kid was delaying the inevitable on purpose. An impatient man was a careless man; the Kid would want the extra edge.

Suddenly, the Kid's demeanor changed drastically. His handsome features grew as flinty as quartz, and his voice acquired steely tension. "Your insults, bastards, will cost you dearly. I might have let you turn around and walk out if you had only insulted me. But no. You did as El Gato instructed you and struck at my weak spot. For that, the time you have left to live can be measured in seconds."

Ramon and Lopez were not intimidated. On the contrary, Ramon chuckled and responded, "El Gato also told us that you love to hear yourself speak, and he was not exaggerating. He also warned us that you are fast, boy. But so are we. Two of the fastest in all northern Mexico. That is why he sent for us. That is why he is paying us so much. Half in advance, the rest when we cut off your right hand and bring it to him."

"My hand?"

"Your gun hand," Lopez said. "The one you killed his brother with."

"No more damn talk!" Ramon cried, tensing with his own hands above the smooth butts of his twin pistols. "Draw, pup. Whenever you are ready. Because no matter how fast you are, you can only get one of us. The other will drop you."

Skye Fargo could not say exactly what made him do what he did next. He owed the Durango Kid no allegiance. Maybe it was that deep down he saw a little of himself in the Kid. Maybe it was because he had never been able to stand idly by when others were in trouble. Whatever the excuse, he stepped away from the bar and lowered his own arms, saying in Spanish, "Kid, you take Lopez. I will take Ramon."

The *pistoleros* did not like the new development, and it showed. Exchanging glances, they studied Fargo and did not seem to like what they saw. Ramon jerked his head to the side and barked, "Go find a woman to bed, fool."

"This does not concern you, *gringo*," Lopez added. "Do not meddle."

Fargo took a casual step to the right so he was directly in front of Ramon. "You should have left when you could. You came a long way just to die."

Quiet descended, a terrible quiet that grated on nerves, the awful lull before the storm. Ramon and Lopez were old hands at this. Now that the gauntlet had been thrown down, they were as immobile as statues, girding themselves for the moment of truth.

Fargo dared not take his eyes off Ramon to check on the Kid. De Leon was on his own. He could only hope that the Kid's reputation was deserved. Instinct and experience warned him that the two *pistoleros* were every bit as deadly as they made themselves out to be. El Gato had hired the best money could buy. Professional assassins who slew without qualm for top dollar. Gun hands tested by countless gunfights. Gunmen with few equals.

It was Ramon who set the explosion off. Liquid lightning, his fingers wrapped around his pistols. Out they flashed, too fast for the human eye to follow.

Fargo was not caught napping. At the very instant that Ramon's hands dipped, so did his. Muscles honed to a razor's edge produced the Colt in less time than it would take a man to blink. He beat Ramon by a fraction of a second. Curling back the hammer as he cleared leather, he fired. The heavy slug smashed into Ramon's chest and jolted the *pistolero* backward, but Ramon did not go down. The killer was forged of iron. Absorbing the shock, Ramon brought up his revolvers. Fargo fired again, a heartbeat before Ramon did. Lead buzzed past an ear. Something snatched at the fringe on his left sleeve. Ramon staggered but did not fall. Game to the last, the gunman attempted to level his pistols again. Fargo put a third slug into him as Ramon raised them, put a fourth slug into him as Ramon swayed as if drunk, a fifth slug as Ramon's knees buckled and the *pistolero* oozed to the floor like a lump of human wax.

It all happened so incredibly quick. Fargo had dimly been aware of firing to his right, of Lopez and the Durango Kid swapping lead. Now he spun, reaching for cartridges to replace those in his spent Colt. Only there was no need.

Lopez lay half across a card table, a pink hole in his forehead, a red one at the base of his throat, a third in the center of his sternum. Convulsions seized him. Shaking violently, he melted onto the floor, his revolvers falling with loud *thunks*.

The Durango Kid stood stock-still, smoke curling from the muzzle of his revolver. A thin crease on his right cheek leaked scarlet drops. Eyes locked on Lopez, he grimaced as if in pain. Then, with a flourish, he twirled the pistol into his holster as expertly as Fargo could have done. "How fragile life is, eh, *compañero?* A minute ago they were as you and I. Now they are husks, fit only for the worms."

Fargo began reloading. Over a third of the customers were Mexicans. One might be working for El Gato, there to witness the encounter and report back to his master. Or maybe finish the job the *pistoleros* had botched. "We should leave."

"What for? I am not done with my bottle yet." The Kid filled his glass and downed it in a gulp. "The bartender will drag those curs out. Come. Let me buy you another round. It is the least I can do after the great favor you have done me."

Against his better judgment, Fargo finished reloading and moved to the bar. Whispers had broken out, soon rising to excited exclamations as the patrons gathered around the corpses. The Durango Kid poured more whiskey into Fargo's glass and offered it to him. "What will you do now?"

"About El Gato? There is not much I can do, my friend. His lair in the mountains is impossible to find. So I must wait for him to come to me. And as you can see, he is not likely to come himself when he can send hirelings to do his dirty work."

"He must hate you a lot."

"That is an understatement. His real name is Joaquin Hernandez. He had a brother by the name of Ignacio, a brute who took delight in making weaker men dance to the tune of bullets fired at their feet, and in beating women when he was drunk. Ignacio was the terror of Durango, Mexico, until one night he imposed himself on a *señorita* I was fond of. One thing led to another and he drew on me. Which was stupid for someone so slow. Since then, Joaquin has lived and breathed hatred for me. He vowed to see me dead, and tried several times before I came back home."

Fargo had a thought. "Wanda told me that Mexican soldiers chased El Gato north of the border. Is that true, or did he come after you?"

"A little of both, I suspect. Joaquin lost track of me after

I left Durango. Somehow or other, though, he learned my true identity and where my family could be found."

It could not be mere coincidence, Fargo mused, that The Cat had been making life miserable for the people of that region ever since. Or that El Gato had struck at the de Leon *hacienda* on several occasions. No, it was plain now that Joaquin Hernandez had embarked on a systematic campaign of vengeance against Alonzo, Alonzo's family, and everyone who lived in the territory. El Gato believed in an eye for an eye. Or, in this case, gallons of blood to make up for the loss of Ignacio. "Have you mentioned this to anyone besides me?"

"No. Why would I? It is something I must deal with on my own."

"But a lot of innocent people have suffered because of it. And a lot more will unless El Gato is stopped."

"If I knew where to find him, I would end it tomorrow," the Kid stated. "But I am no tracker."

Fargo was. Not for nothing did men call him the Trailsman. From the Sioux he had learned the basics of the craft. From skilled scouts and frontiersmen at army posts and elsewhere he had learned more, polishing his ability until he could track better than any man alive. If anyone could locate The Cat's sanctuary, it was him. There was only one catch. In order to track man or beast, a tracker needed a trail of prints, preferably a fresh one. For Fargo to succeed where everyone else had failed, El Gato must strike again. Or be lured into showing himself. He thought of the family Wanda had mentioned, the father and son slain, the mother and daughter raped. On the spur of the moment he came to a decision. "I'm going after Hernandez myself. You're welcome to tag along if you want."

The Kid was tipping his glass to his lips. He looked up in surprise, then set it down. "You are a strange one, *señor*. Why involve yourself? El Gato is no threat to you. Take my advice and ride on."

"Will you help me?"

Grinning wryly, the Kid swallowed some whiskey. "Is it me, or are your ears plugged with wax? Your confidence amazes me. Do you really think you can do what all the farmers and ranchers could not?"

"If you want to end it, one way or the other, meet me at the Howard place at first light. Bring enough grub and coffee to last seven to ten days. It shouldn't take longer than that."

The Kid lost his grin. "The Howard place, you say?"

"Do you know where it is?"

"I think I could find it, yes." The Kid coughed. "Am I to take it that you are staying there tonight?"

"Yes."

The young gunman pulled the sombrero's brim down so that it hid his eyes. "That is most interesting," he said. "Might I ask how that came about? If I am not prying, of course, *amigo*."

"Wanda invited me."

"Did she now?" The Kid grew red in the cheeks. Grasping the bottle, he gulped a few times, then put it down with a loud smack. "That woman. I tell you, she can be a pain. Watch yourself around her. If she gets her claws into you, there will be no prying them out again. She is a witch."

Puzzled, Fargo asked, "Know her well, do you?"

Recovering his composure, the Kid shrugged. "Well enough, I suppose. This is a small community, *señor*. Everyone knows a lot about everyone else. For instance, you might question why a woman as pretty as Wanda has not married. It is because no man will have her. Who wants to share his bed with a wildcat, eh?"

Fargo did not answer. Personally, he was partial to wildcats. They made life, and lovemaking, entertaining. He recollected the time in Denver when a dove had torn his back to ribbons, but every scratch had been worth it. "What about her sister, Clarice?"

The Kid swallowed more rotgut. "What about her?"

"Is she a wildcat, too?"

"I would not know," the Kid said stiffly. "Talking about ladies behind their backs is not a habit I cultivate. My *madre* was a stickler for proper manners."

Fargo covered his mouth to hide a smile. So Wanda was

a pain, but Clarice was a lady? Commotion behind him brought him around to find the bodies being carried from the premises. The bartender oversaw the operation, holding the door wide so the men could file through. Meanwhile, the rest of the customers huddled at tables and along the walls, *anywhere* except near the end of the bar shared by Fargo and the Kid. "We're not very popular at the moment," he commented.

"I never have been," the Kid said. "It is the same everywhere. Those who live by the gun are shunned by those who live by the plow and the rope." He gazed around the room. "Never once have I done any of these men harm, yet they despise me and fear me. They spread all manner of vicious lies about things I have not done. Their wives avoid me on the street. Daughters are whisked away as if I have the plague." The Kid looked as sad as a puppy that had lost a bone. "It is a lonely life, being a *pistolero.*"

"If you feel that way, why don't you go back to your father's *hacienda?*"

"He would like that, *mi padre.* For many months he has begged me to come back. My room is always open, he says. My place at the table is always there." The Kid coughed again, louder, and helped himself to yet more red-eye. "But if I go, it will prove to him that I was wrong to ever leave. It will confirm what he has been saying all along."

A father and son at odds. Age locking horns with youth. Wisdom pitted against pride. It was an age-old struggle, relived countless times. Fargo had seen it all before. And the only ones who could resolve the struggle were the two parties involved. Straightening, he said, "I'm obliged for the drinks. I hope to see you at the Howard place in the morning."

"I might be there. I might not." The Kid gestured at the men who were shunning them. "But there is something I must know first. Are you doing this for me? For them? Or just because you are *loco?*"

"Maybe I'm doing it for myself," Fargo said. A heavy-set townsman scuttled away when he headed for the door. Another man, a farmer, averted his face. A taint was on him. A stigma. Being friendly with the Kid had made him a social outcast in the eyes of the upstanding citizens of Animas City.

Outdoors, Ramon and Lopez were being draped over their horses, distinguished by ornate Mexican saddles. The bartender was rummaging through their saddlebags. Closing one of the flaps, he declared in disgust, "Paid in advance, isn't that what they claimed? Hell, they must have hid it somewhere."

"So we bury 'em cheap," piped up a townsman. "Dig a hole, dump 'em in, and be done with it."

"What about their gear? And their horses?" asked another.

"We'll have Harry auction them off and use the money for the new schoolhouse," suggested someone else.

Fargo did not linger. Crossing to the livery, he removed the Ovaro from the stall. From the tack room he took his saddle and saddle blanket and threw them on the pinto. Last, he secured his bedroll. As he was finishing up, in came Wanda.

"I just heard about the gunfight."

Reins in hand, Fargo walked to the opening. "Does your invitation still hold?"

"Why did you do it, Skye? Why did you help that son of a bitch? Those gun-sharks would have rid us of the Kid once and for all. You shouldn't have butted in." Wanda looked mad enough to take up where Harve Porter had left off. "I sure had you pegged wrong."

"I couldn't stand there and let Alonzo be shot down just to keep him from courting your sister."

Wanda reacted as if she had been slapped. "You know? How? Did he own up to it?"

What should he tell her? Fargo reflected. That the truth had been gleaned from a variety of clues? Such as Clarice being at the canyon at the same time as the Kid. Such as how the Kid behaved whenever the subject of Clarice was brought up. Even Wanda's own unjustified spite.

She glared at the saloon. "Damn him! Until he came along, Clarice was always so sensible. She planned to go

East to school, make something of herself, be a journalist. Now she's on the verge of throwing her dream away. All because of a hankering to run off with that no-account gunman." Wanda clucked like an irate hen. "What she sees in him, I'll never know. But I won't let him ruin her life as he's ruined his own. The only way they will wed is over my dead body."

"Aren't you being a little harsh?"

"Who are you to judge? She's my younger sister, and our parents are dead. I have a responsibility to look after her welfare." Wanda stared at the steps that led up to the doctor's office. "Lucas disagrees. He doesn't think there's any harm in it. So he sneaks Clarice all over creation to meet the Kid." She wrung her hands. "It's wrong of me, I know. But I'm almost glad that Lucas will be laid up for a spell. He can't cover for her now. Once I get home, I'm not letting her out of my sight. It's not too late to nip her romance in the bud."

Hatred appeared to be the rule, not the exception, in Animas City. "Do that, and you run the risk of having her hate you for the rest of your life."

"So? Better her hate me than have her be stuck with a man who isn't fit to lick her shoes clean."

Fargo was seeing a side of Wanda Howard he did not particularly care for. "We'll forget the invitation," he said.

"No!" Wanda clutched his arm and pulled it close, so close that it nestled between her ample breasts. "Please. Forgive me. I must sound like a shrew. But I can't help myself. Clarice is too young to realize the mistake she is making." Wanda pulled him toward the hitching post where her zebra dun had been tied, her hands wrapped tight as if afraid to let go for fear he would go elsewhere. "I promise you. Not another word about the Kid. Say you'll come?"

Perhaps it was the whiskey. Or perhaps Fargo had been on the trail too long. Whatever the case, the contact of his arm against her jiggling mounds was enough to stir his manhood to full attention. His tongue felt thick, his throat constricted. "I'll go," he said.

"Wonderful!" Clapping her hands in glee, Wanda ran to the zebra dun.

Mounting the Ovaro, Fargo rode beside her northward out of town. Soon Animas City was a collection of lights to their rear, and they were among the cabins and frame homes belonging to its residents. Dogs yapped at them from yards and porches. Curtains were parted and faces peered suspiciously out. Once a man bearing a shotgun stepped to a front gate to scrutinize them as they went by. Only when Wanda bid him good evening did he relax and smile.

Fargo had met some unfriendly folks in his wide-flung travels. The close-knit clans of the Appalachians were always suspicious of strangers. In the deep South, Southerners were mistrustful of anyone who hailed from north of the Mason and Dixon Line. The dwellers of the bayou country wanted nothing to do with outsiders. But none of them could hold a candle to the good people of Animas City. Even allowing for the ever-present threat of being raided by El Gato, they were distrustful and cold to the point of being downright hostile.

The Howard cabin turned out to be one of the farthest from town, a quaint home situated beside a bubbling creek and surrounded on three sides by a grove of trees. A small barn, a corral, and an outhouse were evidence of the pride that Wanda's father had taken in the homestead. Light glowed from two windows. On a narrow porch sat a rocking chair. As Fargo and Wanda trotted up, from under the porch padded a large black dog with a white throat. It growled and crouched, baring teeth half the size of the grizzly's. Fargo's hand automatically strayed to his Colt, but Wanda called the dog off.

"Brutus! That's enough out of you. This is a friend. You hear me? I don't want you to take a bite out of him like you did that patent medicine man."

"Brutus?" Fargo said.

"It's from some play my father liked," Wanda explained. "Written by an English guy. I never could remember what

58

it was called." Swinging both legs over the saddle, she dropped to the ground.

The front door opened, spilling more light into the yard. Clarice was framed in the doorway, armed with a rifle. "Oh. It's just you," she said on seeing her sister, then she realized that Wanda was not alone. "Mr. Fargo! You made it back safe and sound!" Dashing down the steps, she rushed over and embraced him as soon as he stepped from the stirrups. "My grandpa owes his life to you. We'll never forget what you did for us. Never."

Compared to Wanda's prickly disposition, the younger woman's innocence and sincerity were like a gust of bracing wind. Fargo could see why Alonzo de Leon favored her, and why she favored him. "Your sister agreed to put me up for the night. Hope I won't be a bother."

"None whatsoever," Clarice assured him. She glanced at the cabin and gasped. "Goodness gracious! I forgot. We weren't expecting company. The place is a mess. And I was fixing on having leftover pork rinds for supper."

Wanda moved behind Clarice and steered her toward the porch. "I'll tell you what, little sister. You sweep out the house and prepare a pot of stew while I show our guest where to bed his horse."

"All right." Clarice scooted to the doorway. "But keep him out there a while. Our unmentionables are scattered all over the place. I'll need at least half an hour."

"Oh, no problem there," Wanda said dryly. After the door closed, she warmly clasped Fargo's hand to lead him to the barn. A single wide door opened onto a row of four stalls, a feed trough, and a hay loft. In the front stall was a plow horse, in the rear stall a cow.

"That's Bessie," Wanda said. "I brought her in for safe-keeping. She's about to drop a calf and I didn't want the mountain lions or wolves to get it. Our neighbor lost a prize foal to a big cat last year."

So there was a soft side to her, after all. She rambled on about the plot her father had filed on and the big plans they had for it, while Fargo unsaddled the pinto. He caught her watching his every move. When he threw his bedroll across his shoulder and turned, she smiled coyly.

"No need for that, handsome. We have a spare bed."

Her hands behind her back, Wanda sashayed up to him and gazed impishly into his eyes. "Mercy me," she said. "Clarice needs half an hour, and here we have another twenty minutes to kill. However should we pass the time?"

Fargo was not given a chance to answer. Wanda's slim hands rose up around his neck and she molded her full body against him, her breath tingling his lips as she passionately joined their mouths. For the second time that evening, Fargo's manhood swelled. And this time he was going to do something about it.

5

Fargo had to keep in mind that they did not have much time. Clarice might blunder into the barn at any moment. Placing both hands on Wanda's bottom, he pressed her against his groin. She felt his hunger and groaned deep in her throat. Her mouth parted to admit his tongue. As he glided it over her teeth, her tongue met his halfway to entwine in a silken dance. Her breathing grew husky with desire, and she clung to his broad shoulders as if afraid her legs were too weak to support her on their own.

His right hand roamed to the small of her back, halfway up her spine, then around to the front. At the first contact of his palm with her breast, Wanda arched her body and mashed her mouth against him so hard, it actually hurt. She sucked on his tongue, inhaling it, her fingernails biting into him. When he squeezed her glorious mound, she cooed like a dove. When he tweaked her hardening nipple, she ground herself into him with renewed ardor. She gave him the impression that she had not shared herself with a man in quite a while, and she was hankering to make up for the lack.

Fargo would have liked to dally at her breast, to slowly stroke her inner furnace, to draw out the experience for them to savor. Lovemaking was a lot like a campfire in that regard. Both should be made hotter by gradual degrees. A man kindled a tiny flame into bigger ones, fanning them and adding fuel until he had a roaring fire going. But in this case they were denied the luxury of extra time. At the back of his mind was the constant thought that Clarice would soon be done and come to see what was keeping them.

Without further foreplay, he cupped both of Wanda's

swelling mounds. They were magnificent, thrusting outward from her lush body like twin flowers from a stem, as big as melons and softer than down-filled pillows. Slipping a hand lower, he tugged at the bottom of her shirt, freeing it so he could slide his fingers up and under. Her skin rippled to his touch. Kneading it, he roved upward until he made contact with a breast.

Fargo massaged her with growing urgency. He worked the rigid nipple between his thumb and forefinger. At the same time he unfastened the buttons to her shirt. When the garment parted, out popped her generous globes. They were exquisite. Carnal hunger filled him, and he lowered his mouth to one. Her skin was salty to the taste, her nipple extremely sensitive to his swirling tongue.

"Oh, yes. I've been dreaming of this all day."

Had she indeed? Fargo gave her other breast the same treatment. It set her legs to wriggling and elicited several moans. She closed her eyes and lifted her head to the beams above. Wanda had no idea his other hand had dropped to the junction of her thighs. She nearly jumped when his hand poked between them and brushed her boiling core.

"Ahhhhhh! Like that!"

Fargo was glad she approved. He rubbed her through the fabric, rubbing faster and faster and harder and harder, the friction increasing the heat and adding to her pleasure. She squeezed both thighs against his hand and shook as if having convulsions. Tossing her head from side to side, she huffed like a runner who had sprinted a mile.

To the right, in an empty stall, was a pile of clean straw. Fargo steered Wanda toward it, an arm around her waist to keep her from falling. She stumbled along as if drunk, lost in the delirium of raw lust, as easy to manipulate as putty when he pulled her down onto her back. Lying alongside her, he renewed his acquaintance with her breasts. Kissing and tweaking and lathering them, he unhooked her pants and pushed them lower, down around her knees.

Much to Fargo's surprise, Wanda did not have any underthings on. He ran a palm over her bushy thatch to the edge of her nether mound. She gurgled and smacked her cherry red lips, spreading her legs to make access easier. Extending his forefinger, Fargo probed her depths. Her womanhood was hot and moist, the petals yielding at the slightest pressure. Before he knew it, his finger was imbedded to the knuckle in her inner well.

"Ohhhhhhh! Yes!"

Fargo only had to move his finger a fraction to provoke her into clutching him and grinding her posterior against his hand. He stroked his finger out, then in, again and again, matching the tempo of her movement. Wanda cried out, then bit her lower lip to keep from doing so again. Moving between her legs, he loosened his gun belt and his pants. He had to resist an urge to explore her core further, to nuzzle into her like someone bobbing for apples. There was Clarice to think of. Always Clarice. His organ slid out, engorged. Wanda saw it, her eyes widening, her tongue greedily rimming her mouth.

"So big! You're a stallion!"

She wrapped a hand around the base. It was Fargo's turn to groan, to close his eyes as she did things to him that set his blood to racing and sharp tingles to shooting up his spine. A nail traced a delicate path from bottom to top and back again. She cupped him, lower down, and he feared for a few moments that he would explode before he was ready. An amused smile spread across her flushed face. She knew exactly what she was doing to him, knew that she was driving him crazy.

Remember Clarice, Fargo's mind prodded. Suddenly pushing her legs wider, Fargo bent. Wanda guided him to her slit. A rocking motion of his knees, and the deed was done. His pulsing sword was buried in her sheath. She gripped his arms, digging into him, the amusement replaced by ecstasy.

"Do me. Please."

Fargo was happy to oblige. But as he started to heave into her, he thought that he heard a sound outside. Glancing at the door, he saw no one. Propping his hands on either side of Wanda, he settled into a steady rhythm. She accommodated him by holding onto his hips and thrusting outward when he thrust in. Their mutual tempo soon brought them to the brink. A lump formed in Fargo's throat. His whole body seemed to hum like a taut guitar string. An ache in his loins let him know that release was not far off.

Another noise snapped his head around. The barn was empty, the patch of yard that he could see was deserted. Yet he could not shake a nagging conviction that someone was out there, possibly spying on them.

Let them, Fargo reflected. He was not about to stop. Not now. Not even if Clarice were to enter. His inner fuse had burned down to the wick, and his charge was on the verge of exploding. The world could come to an end, and he wouldn't give a damn.

Kissing Wanda, he gripped both breasts. She panted and ripped skin from his arms. Her thighs closed around him, her ankles locking behind his back. They were glued at the lips and at the hips, the two of them made one. Every downward surge of his was met by an upward surge of equal force from her. Like two waves flowing into one another, they were a rolling surf of sensual sensation. Fargo's release was imminent when Wanda abruptly clawed him harder and raised them both up out of the straw.

"Skye! I'm coming! I'm coming!"

Wanda's well gushed, her eyes fluttered, her body was as hot as fireplace coals. Her tongue filled his mouth, seeking to plunge down his throat. Her nipples were spikes, her belly smacking his in a frenzy. He had breached the last of her inner walls, and now her inhibitions came crashing down. She was pure passion incarnate, a wildcat unleashed.

Fargo rode the crest, slamming his battering ram into her over and over. The blast came, his manhood seeming to burst at the tip. His vision briefly blurred. All he could hear was the hammering of his heart. Vaguely, he sensed that someone was in the doorway to the barn, watching them. He tried to turn, to look, but his body refused to respond. His mind was mush. Ablaze with the white light of a veil he could not pierce, he coasted to a gradual stop. Only then did his brain clear, his senses return in full. He twisted, but no one else was present. Either it had been his imagination, or whoever it was had gone.

As much as Fargo would have liked to lie down and doze, he rose onto his knees and put himself in order. His hat had fallen off. Donning it, he stood, his legs a little spongy until he flexed them and took a few steps. Wanda lay in a daze, her eyes glazed, wearing a contented smile. "You should get dressed," he suggested.

"Ummmmmm," she said, making no attempt to sit up.

Fargo leaned down and shook her shoulder. "Your sister, remember? Our twenty minutes are about up."

Wanda blinked, and was on her feet the next second. Hurriedly arranging her clothes, she grinned at him and said, "Thanks, handsome. I hope we can get together again before you leave our neck of the country."

"Any time," Fargo promised. She took a step and tilted her head to kiss him, but froze with her lips puckered, fright lining her countenance. Whatever had scared her was at the front of the barn. Pivoting, he began to go for his Colt, but a mocking snicker—and the twin muzzles of a sawed-off shotgun—turned him into marble.

"Very smart of you, *gringo*," said the Mexican who held the scattergun. He and his companion were cut from the same coarse cloth as Lopez and Ramon. The other man had thrown back a *serape* and held a Smith & Wesson in either hand. Stubble covered their chins, and their hair was long and unwashed.

Wanda fanned her courage. "What is the meaning of this outrage? What do you want?"

The bandit with the scattergun stepped to the right so he was out of the doorway and no one could see him from outside. His friend moved to the left. "Be careful how you talk to us, *señorita*," said the first man. "We were not told to harm you. Should you give us trouble, though, El Gato said we may tie you up and stuff a gag in your mouth."

"El Gato?" Wanda said, and swallowed hard. "The men in Animas City will do all in their power to bring him to justice if you harm my sister or me."

The first man chuckled. "They have done all in their

power many times, have they not? And we are still at large." He leaned back against the wall. "The whites here are weak, *señorita*, weak and stupid. They could not find us if we painted signs giving them directions."

At this, the other gunman laughed, a low, guttural sound, like the grating of stone on stone.

"See. Pedro agrees," said the first one. "Now, you will tell us where he is, or this will get most unpleasant."

Wanda was perplexed. "Where who is?"

"Who else? Alonzo de Leon. The Durango Kid." The man with the shotgun held up a hand when she went to speak. "Do not lie to me, *señorita*. Do not pretend you don't know him. A little mouse has whispered in El Gato's ear and confided that your sister and the Kid are, how shall we say, *estan enamorado*? They are very close, no?"

"Too damn close," Wanda retorted. "He and I are hardly the best of friends. If I had any idea, I'd tell you just-like-that." She snapped her fingers to accent her point.

The man scratched his chin. "This is most interesting. You hate him, I take it? El Gato and you have something in common. Be that as it may, though, we are not leaving until we have done as we were ordered. Perhaps you can—"

Footsteps outside silenced him. Wanda opened her mouth to shout, but the *pistolero* holding the Smith & Wessons pointed them at her and cocked both hammers. Into the barn ran Clarice, smiling merrily, unaware of the two men in the shadows. "I'm done cleaning, and stew is on the stove," she announced.

Fargo had not taken his eyes off the bandits. If the man using the scattergun would only lower it for a few seconds, he would go for his Colt. But no such luck. Both gunmen stepped into the open, the first man keeping those twin muzzles fixed on his chest.

Clarice spotted them and stifled a scream by stuffing the back of a hand into her mouth. Backpedaling to her sister, she clutched Wanda's arm.

"Ah, the one we were looking for," the first man said. "The one with hair like the sun. *Señorita*, I am Varga. I do the bidding of the man you call The Cat. He would very

66

much like to talk to the Durango Kid. Tell me. Is the Kid in the *casa?* In your house?"

Clarice took her hand from her mouth. "No, he's not. And if he were, I'd scream to warn him. Go away and let us be."

Pedro glanced at Varga and said in Spanish, "These Americans never cease to amaze me. They are so childish, the men and women alike. Let me use my knife on her. She will tell us everything we need to know."

In Spanish Varga responded, "What if you get carried away, like that time down in Sonora? She is of no use to us dead. But alive, she is the cheese that will bring the mouse into our trap."

"And her sister and the *gringo?* Shall I shoot them? They are of no use."

Varga sidled toward the opening. "I would say yes, but what if de Leon is on his way here? We were told he visits nearly every night about this time. He might hear the shots and stay away."

"I can slit their throats quietly enough," Pedro said.

"Later. The *gringo* might resist and force us to use our guns. Tie them up for now and put them in the back. We will take the younger sister to the house and eat some of that stew she mentioned while we wait."

"*Sí.*"

In short order Fargo was stripped of his gun belt, his wrists were bound, and he was hustled to a rear corner where his ankles were also tied. Wanda was next. She balked and argued, earning a slap from Pedro that rocked her on her heels. Cowed, she submitted to being trussed up and dumped beside Fargo. They were securely gagged. Finally, Pedro brought a blanket and covered them, giving them both a parting kick before he walked off.

Muffled but clear enough to make out, Fargo heard Varga say, "Now *señorita*, you will take us to the *casa*. No tricks, or I will have my friend come back with the knife he carries in his boot. Your *hermana*, your sister and her friend, will be cut into small pieces, and left to rot."

The barn became quiet. Fargo tested the ropes, fingered

the knots. Pedro had done an outstanding job. It would hold most men. But Pedro and Varga had been careless. They had not checked Fargo from head to toe, or they would have discovered that Pedro was not the only one who had a hidden blade.

Wanda was shifting and kicking at the blanket. After it fell off them, she turned and offered her arms. When he did not do anything, she glared and scolded him, her words distorted by the gag.

Fargo let her rave on. Tucking at the waist, he curled his legs behind him so his fingers could slip into his right boot. It took some doing. The boot fit tightly, and his arms were at an uncomfortable angle, but at length he had the hilt of his Arkansas toothpick in hand and slid it out. Wanda stopped chiding him. Pumping her arms, she said what sounded like, "Do it! Do it! Do it!"

Slicing the ropes took a while, longer than Fargo liked. He figured that as soon as he was done with her, she would repay the favor. To his dismay, however, Wanda shoved upright and dashed toward the doorway. She did not even bother to remove the gag. He called her name, or tried to, but she ran from the building without a backward glance. In her anxiety over her sister, she had left him to fend for himself. And in doing so, she had likely doomed all of them. Alone, she was no match for the gunmen.

With not a moment to spare, Fargo reversed his grip on the toothpick and sawed at the loops around his wrists. The urgency drove him to be reckless. Twice he nicked a wrist, three times he cut a finger. The pain and the blood did not upset him half as much as the thought of Wanda being caught. Varga would not run the risk of their escaping a second time.

Craning his neck to determine how much more he had to do, Fargo nearly missed the dull *clomp* of a hoof. A rider was approaching. Was it the Kid? he wondered. Or someone passing by? Desperately, he sawed the blade back and forth, cramps in his fingers and wrists adding to the misery. Just when he felt that he could not endure another moment, the ropes gave way.

Elated, Fargo stood. His fingers dripped blood, and his palms were slick. He had to wipe them to grip the toothpick firmly. Hastening to the wide door, he inched an eye to the edge. The yard was deceptively tranquil. Close to the house was the zebra dun, cropping at grass. A shadow passed across the window. By the silhouette, it was Clarice.

Fargo turned and ran to his saddle. He had left the Henry in the boot; now the boot was empty. Foiled, he sought another way out of the barn. There was none, although the outline of a rear door had been traced in chalk on the planks—a project never finished by the sisters' father.

Returning to the door, Fargo crouched and angled toward a tree to the left. Shielded by the trunk, he listened for the sound of the rider. The hoofbeats had died. He surveyed the property for some sign of Wanda, but she was gone. Then, as he was rising to run to another tree closer to the house, he sensed that he was no longer alone. Spinning, he brought the knife up to throw.

It was only Brutus. The huge hound stared at him, tongue lolling. It did not growl or act otherwise unfriendly. Fargo motioned for it to go away, but instead it walked toward him, sniffing. He had nowhere to run if it should attack. Lowering his empty hand so the dog could smell it, he whispered, "Nice fella. Remember me?"

Apparently Brutus did. The dog touched a damp nose to Fargo's palm, sneezed, and sank onto its hindquarters. Unsure what it wanted, and afraid it might attract the attention of Varga and Pedro, Fargo shooed it off, whispering, "Scat! Go find a bone to chew on."

Brutus would not budge.

Shrugging, Fargo faced the cabin. Short of driving it off with a stick and raising a ruckus, he had to accept its presence for the time being. Low to the ground, he sprinted to the other tree. From here he could see the front porch plainly, as well as the other window. Presently another female silhouette appeared. Was Varga making Clarice move around to give the illusion all was well?

Fargo glanced in the direction of the road. A man on horseback would be obvious, and he saw no one. Moving around the trunk, he prepared to bolt to the porch. An object poking against the back of his leg brought him up short. Automatically, he whirled, the Arkansas toothpick rising.

It was the dog again. Brutus rubbed against him, then licked his arm. For such a big dog, Brutus was a kitten. Fargo had half a mind to kick it, but the yelp was bound to be heard. Patting its neck, he started past the tree, halting in midstep when the front door was flung wide.

Framed between the jambs was Pedro. Pistols at the ready, he came to the end of the porch and scoured the area. Fargo hugged the trunk, grateful for the shadow that hid him. He was confident he would not be detected. Then Brutus woofed softly and stepped into the open. Pedro swung toward the tree, the Smith & Wessons centering on the dog.

Again Brutus uttered a low woof. Pedro gestured in disgust and hissed, "*Estupido perro!*" His attitude left no doubt he would love to put lead into the animal, but after a string of obscenity, Pedro backed into the house and closed the door.

Brutus growled and pawed at the ground.

Fargo agreed wholeheartedly. He took a partial step, stopping dead when a curtain moved. Part of a face appeared, no more than a nose and an eyebrow, but enough to identify who was peering out. Clarice was the only one in there who did not have a mustache. She gazed toward the road until a hand clamped onto her shoulder and yanked her back.

The southwest corner was the darkest. Fargo jogged there, favoring the shadows, using the available cover to the fullest. As he ran around to the side, he collided with someone coming the other way. A hand grabbed his wrist, another clawed at his neck. He braced to land a punch, a punch not thrown when he caught a minty fragrance.

Past him streaked Brutus, to leap up on the other figure and rake a slavering tongue over her face and neck. "No, Brutus!" Wanda said. "Down, boy! Get down!"

"Quiet!" Fargo directed. She was making enough noise to alert the gunmen, and half her neighbors, besides. The creak of a hinge from out front sparked him into clamping a hand over her mouth and pushing her against the wall. Wanda struggled for a moment, calming when he whispered in her ear, "They've heard you, damn it."

Cautiously, Fargo took a look. A rectangle of light in front of the porch confirmed the door was open. In the center of the rectangle was the murky outline of a man. Pedro again, Fargo guessed. The shadow in the rectangle grew larger. Down the steps walked the two-gun killer. Glancing right and left, he headed left, away from them. At the far corner he tramped from sight. Fargo started. The *pistolero* was making a circuit of the house! "We must hide. One of them is coming."

Wanda snatched his hand and bolted toward a shed. Brutus loped along beside them, bouncing playfully. They ducked behind it, and Wanda threw both arms around the dog to keep him from straying off. Brutus whined and kicked, but she held on.

Fargo flattened, removed his hat, and checked on Pedro. It was a full thirty seconds before the gunman walked around the northwest corner and ambled to the front, passing the very spot they had occupied. Striding to the porch, he scowled and scoured the night one last time. The slam of the door spooked the zebra dun, which tugged at its reins and tried to run off.

Brutus was behaving himself. Wanda released him, but held onto his thick leather collar. "What now?" she whispered. "We have to get my sister out of there before the Kid shows up. I don't want her caught in the cross fire."

Neither did Fargo. "Is there a rear door?"

"No. Pa was going to add another room and put in one to the back yard, but he died before we could get up the money for the lumber."

"Any windows?"

"One. To my ma's old room. I always keep it shuttered and locked to prevent Clarice from sneaking out to see the Kid."

Fargo was at his wit's end. Short of setting the log structure on fire, he had no means of driving the bandits out and no way of disposing of them if he did. His gaze roved to the barn, to a nearby garden, to a pile of rocks next to it. "Stay put. If I go down, sneak out of here and fetch help." He rose, replacing his hat.

"Wait a minute. Brutus and I can help. He'll go after them if I say the word."

It was food for thought. The dog might distract the *pistoleros* long enough for Fargo to bring one of them down, scoop up a revolver, and save everyone's hide. But in the process, Brutus was bound to absorb a few slugs. The bandits did not pack all that hardware for bluff or balance. They were extremely proficient gun handlers, or they would not be part of El Gato's band. "No. Keep the dog with you for protection."

Fargo took several swift strides, gaining speed. He was ten feet from the shed when the front door opened again. Unable to retrace his steps without being seen, he dived onto his stomach in the high grass. Pedro came out again, but this time he was not alone. The gunman had Clarice by the arm. She was gagged and blindfolded and hurting, to judge by how she hung her head and by her shuffling gait. Pedro led her to the tree close to the house and lashed her to it. They were only thirty feet away, tempting Fargo to rise onto his hands and knees. Temptation vanished when Varga strolled onto the porch, the scattergun in the crook of an elbow.

Now what? Fargo asked himself. Why had they changed their minds about laying a trap for the Kid?

Varga answered the question by cupping a hand to his mouth and hollering, "Do you see her, Alonzo? See the *puta?*"

Fargo scanned the yard. What was the *bandito* talking about? The Durango Kid had not shown up yet.

"We know you are out there," Varga called out. "I broke the lock and was watching from the back window when you circled the *casa*. So join the party, half-breed spawn. Or Pedro will cut your pretty *puta* up. Starting with her ample upper charms. They would make excellent pouches, don't you think?"

Convinced Varga was mistaken, that he had heard Brutus and Wanda and jumped to the conclusion the Kid must be close by, Fargo snaked toward Pedro. To throw the toothpick with any degree of accuracy he had to be a lot nearer.

The thump of heavy hooves resounded in the darkness. Out of the woods to the east rode Alonzo de Leon, as casually as if he were on his father's *hacienda*. Smiling broadly, as usual, he came to the opposite end of the porch and drew rein. "You always did have eyes like an eagle, Varga."

"And the brains of a fox," Varga answered. He raised the scattergun. "To be frank, I did not think you would make it this easy. Say your prayers."

6

Skye Fargo did not understand why the Durango Kid made no attempt to save himself. It was a puzzle to ponder later. Both Varga and Pedro had their backs to him. Slowly rising into a crouch, he stalked them. Only Clarice Howard saw him. Tears were streaming down her cheeks, and she was desperately trying to twist toward the Kid, but the ropes hampered her.

Alonzo de Leon wrapped the reins to his horse around his saddle horn, saying, "I made peace with our Maker for my sins long ago. When you are ready, shoot. But I ask a favor first."

"What kind of favor?" Varga asked.

The Kid nodded at the tree. "Let the woman go. *Por favor*. She has never harmed you. She poses no threat to El Gato. I will not resist if you give me your solemn word that she will not be hurt."

Varga had the scattergun tucked to his side. "You would trust me to keep such a promise? When I ride with your bitter enemy?"

"Some people claim no honor exists among *pistoleros*. I know better. Wearing a pistol does not make a man less than he can be unless he allows it to." The Kid rested his hands on top of the horn. "Yes, I will take your word. Whatever else you are, whatever else you have done, you have the look of a man who does not break his pledges."

Pedro snorted. "The young fool. Kill him, Varga, so we can be on our way. I can feel the money El Gato agreed to pay us already jingling in my pocket."

"Be quiet," Varga snapped.

"What has gotten into you?" Pedro would not heed. "Surely you are not thinking of doing what he wants? El Gato will have you skinned alive. You remember what he said. Not only the Kid, but everyone who had ever befriended him, are to die. Horribly."

The Durango Kid slumped. "So. I was afraid of that. Trying to persuade you to spare my sweetheart is a waste of time. To save her I must stay alive."

"As if you have any choice," Pedro taunted.

By then Fargo was ten feet from the two-gun *pistolero*. Cocking his right arm, he took several more steps. Clarice had wide eyes locked on him. Whether the Kid had spotted him, he could not say.

Pedro picked that moment to glance at Clarice. "Did you hear your stupid man, *puta?*" He paused. "What are you looking at like that?" Cocked revolvers held at his waist, he turned.

Fargo struck with the speed of a rattler. His arm flashed, and the Arkansas toothpick cleaved the air, the slim steel glistening in the lantern light from the doorway. It sank into Pedro's chest with a thud, cleaving to the hilt. Pedro staggered backward, bewilderment sapping his will until the reality registered, and he swiveled the Smith & Wessons.

Fargo threw himself to the right as the revolvers boomed. Landing on his shoulder, he rolled, slugs tearing into the soil beside him. Out of the corner of an eye he glimpsed the Kid leaving the saddle in a headlong plunge, the ivory-handled Colt blossoming. It cracked a heartbeat before the scattergun thundered, but Fargo did not see the result. He launched into a series of rolls to spoil Pedro's aim. Five times he rolled, and after the fifth, when he realized that no more shots had been fired, he shoved up onto a knee.

Pedro was seated on the grass, arms limp, the revolvers dangling from fingers that no longer had the strength to hold them. Dumbfounded, he gawked at the knife jutting from his ribs and endeavored to speak. All that issued from his mouth were rivulets of blood.

On the porch, Varga had fallen across the rail. Scarlet

stained his shirt and his beard. The scattergun lay on the ground, smoking from both barrels.

The Durango Kid was picking himself up. His sombrero was gone, lying a dozen feet away, blown half to ribbons by the blast that would have done the same to his head if it had been a few inches lower. "*Compañero!*" he cried cheerfully, running toward the tree. "You have risked your own life to save mine twice this night. How will I ever repay you?" He stopped in front of Clarice and tenderly caressed her face, then kissed her on the forehead. "My love, I could not let them hurt you."

Fargo pulled the toothpick from Pedro. He thought the gunman was still alive, but Pedro's eyes had gone vacant. Wiping the blade clean on the killer's shirt, he quickly freed Clarice. She flung herself at the Kid, wrapping her arms around him and sobbing into his shoulder.

"There, there," Alonzo said. "It is over. Everything is fine."

"Is it?"

A winter gale in the form of Wanda Howard stormed onto the scene. She reached for Clarice to pull her sister away from the Kid, but Alonzo turned so she couldn't. "Let me have her," Wanda fumed.

"When will you accept that we are meant for each other?" the Kid responded. "Go inside. She will join you when she is good and ready."

Wanda was livid. "How many times must we go through this? So long as you make a living by your gun, you're not fit to hold her hand. I won't have you seeing her. I won't risk having her run off with you some night. Living on the go, never having a home, never knowing if you'll live out each day. What kind of life is that?"

Fargo started for the steps. He assumed that was where he would find his Henry and Colt. But the Kid's next statement brought him to a halt on the porch.

"Put your fears to rest, for I have decided to marry her."

It was hard to say whether Wanda or Clarice was more astounded. Wanda looked as if she were trying to catch moths in her mouth. Clarice had straightened and was slinging to the Kid's shoulders.

"You heard correctly," Alonzo informed them. "I will do what is honorable. I will return to my father, beg his forgiveness, and take my rightful place on the *hacienda*. Then there will be the grandest wedding anyone in these parts has ever seen. The celebration will go on for days. And when it is done, your sister will be Clarice de Leon, my wife, my soul."

Wanda groped the air as if seeking a chair to sit in. Failing that, she steadied her legs and said, "If you're sincere, then I have grossly misjudged you."

"Would I lie about a thing like marriage?" the Kid said testily. "All this time I have been telling you that I love your sister, yet still you doubt?" Embracing Clarice, he declared, "Now, at last, everything will be as it should. We will be together always, my love, and you need never fear."

Wanda began to back off, to let them be alone. She nearly tripped when her left foot bumped against Pedro. Looking down, she frowned. "You're forgetting something, aren't you, Alonzo?"

"Eh?" The Kid stared at the *pistolero*.

"So long as El Gato is alive, my sister will always have cause to be afraid," Wanda said. "Marrying you will not set things right. It will make them worse. Because to get at you, El Gato will go after her. He will send more men like these two and the pair who braced you in town. He won't rest until you, and Clarice, are dead."

The Durango Kid could not dispute the truth.

"I can't approve of any wedding until you've settled accounts with The Cat," Wanda said. "Oh, Clarice and you can sneak off and find a preacher somewhere who will tie the knot, but it won't be the same, and we both know it. To do this right, you must prove to me that my sister won't ever be in any danger."

"And how exactly do I do that?" the Kid asked.

"It's simple. Bring me the head of El Gato in a sack, and I will personally have the wedding invitations printed up."

Wanda entered the house, moving past Fargo with her

head bowed. Clarice, who had hardly uttered a word, burst into more tears and was ushered into the darkness by her beau. Fargo located his guns in the living room on a sofa. As he checked the cylinder of the revolver, Wanda walked from a room on the left.

"You must think I'm the worst bitch who ever lived."

"It's not my place to judge," Fargo said. Twirling the Colt into his holster, he hoisted the Henry and made for the door. Her sorrowful expression spurred him to add, "I admit that until a short while ago I thought you were meddling in your sister's life. But after what happened out there . . ." He left the comment unfinished. As he opened the door, Wanda said his name.

"Do you still intend to ride out after El Gato in the morning?"

"Need you ask?"

"Be careful, Skye. He's a sly devil. And you've seen for yourself that he'll stop at nothing to rub out the Kid. Go hunting him and you're hunting trouble with a capital T."

Fargo had a suggestion to offer. "Take your sister into Animas City until it's over. More *pistoleros* might pay you a visit, and the Kid and I won't be able to protect you."

"Will do."

There was no trace of Alonzo de Leon and Clarice. Fargo made himself comfortable in the barn, bedding down in the same pile of hay in which he had made love to Wanda. Covered by a blanket, warm and snug, he slept soundly until the crowing of a rooster awakened him shortly before sunrise. He washed up in the horse trough, saddled the Ovaro, and led the animal out. Someone was waiting for him.

"Are you surprised to see me, *amigo?*" the Durango Kid asked.

"I would have been more surprised if you hadn't shown up," Fargo replied. His saddle creaked as he mounted. The house was quiet. Sparrows flitted in the trees. Chickens pecked at the dirt outside their coop. On a stump perched the rooster, which tossed back its head to crow loudly. The bodies of Varga and Pedro were gone.

The Kid followed the direction of his gaze and said, "I took the liberty of disposing of them. No need to bother the ladies, eh?"

It was a fine morning. The air was crisp and clear. A rosy crown framed the eastern horizon, growing brighter by the minute. Robins hopped about in search of worms. Out on the range, cattle grazed.

Fargo wheeled the pinto to the northwest and clucked it into a brisk walk. The San Juans were a far piece, yet not so far that the distant white caps of snow could not be seen. A pair of twin peaks were the landmarks by which he marked their route. The mountains below those peaks were some of the most rugged and inaccessible in all the Rockies. Logic indicated that El Gato's stronghold was located there, if anywhere.

The Durango Kid was uncommonly silent for most of the day. Not until they pitched camp for the night in a sheltered glen did he open up. "Women are strange creatures, are they not, my friend?" he said between sips of coffee. "They can be so soft and gentle, yet as hard as iron. A mystery, is it not?"

Fargo figured he was talking about Wanda, but he was mistaken.

"Take Clarice. She cried for over an hour last night. Bawled tears until she had no more to shed, holding me the whole time and whispering how much she loved me." The Kid smiled wistfully. "Then, when the tears stopped, she told me that she agreed with her sister. That unless something was done about The Cat, there would be no wedding. Our dream of having a life together would be over." He slapped dust from his pants. "I tried to tell her there is no guarantee we will find El Gato, let alone kill him. I told her that we could still get married, and live on the *hacienda*. My father has many *vaqueros* who will protect us. We would be safe there."

"She didn't go for it."

"No. She did not. She worried that her sister and grandfather would suffer on our account. That if El Gato could not get to us, he would take out his rage on them."

"She's right."

The Kid sighed. "*Sí*. In my head I know that, but in my heart I wish she would take the easy way out." Leaning back against a log he had pulled from the trees a while ago, the Kid adjusted the chin strap to the sombrero he had taken from Varga. "But that has always been my main shortcoming. I have always taken the easy way out. I did not want to spend my life in toil as my father has done. I did not want to earn the good things life has to offer. I believed they would just fall into my lap, like overripe fruit from a tree."

"Live and learn," Fargo remarked.

"Some people never do. Joaquin Hernandez, for instance. He has always been a murdering butcher, and he always will be."

"His butchering days are about over."

"How can you be so sure, *amigo?* Many others have tried to snare him, and they all failed."

"They weren't using the right bait."

"Bait?" the Kid said. He looked at their horses, at their saddles, at their bedrolls, and he laughed. "You must be joking, *señor*. We own little of value. There is nothing here El Gato would possibly be interested in—" Suddenly he stopped, his eyes narrowing. "Wait a minute. You cannot mean what I think you mean."

"Care to bet?" Fargo filled his tin cup with piping hot coffee and allowed himself to relax for the first time since sunrise. "We're not going to try tracking El Gato to his lair. Once he learns you're in the mountains, he'll come to us."

"And how do you propose to let him know where I am?" the Kid asked a trifle anxiously.

"Advertise."

The Kid badgered him, but Fargo would not go into detail. Not that night, not the next day, or the next. By then they were winding steadily up the emerald green foothills to the majestic San Juans. The willows and cottonwoods gave way to evergreens and aspens. Jays and ravens replaced the sparrows and robins. Elk were abundant. At one point, as they crossed a ridge, Fargo saw fresh grizzly tracks. By their size, it could well be the same bear he had clashed with in the lowlands. He was wary the remainder of the day, but the brute never appeared.

"How much higher must we climb?" the Kid wanted to know the next morning after they had been in the saddle over an hour. "I did not think to bring a heavy coat, and I am not immune to the cold night air as you seem to be."

"There's no telling how far up we must go," Fargo said. Based on the information Wanda had provided, he gathered that El Gato's sanctuary had to be a lot higher than any of the search parties had previously gone. It must be in one of the many alpine valleys high up in the rugged vastness to the north. Accordingly, he had been angling northward as well as constantly climbing since they struck the mountains. Sooner or later they would stumble on some sign.

The Kid grumbled, but forged on. About midmorning he broke into song, bawdy *cantina* lyrics not fit to be repeated in mixed company.

It was shortly before noon, as they were traversing a tableland dominated by fir, that Fargo's perseverance paid off. He reined up on the bank of a wide stream to water the horses. Sliding down, he leaned forward to dip a palm into the cold water. Under his very nose was a human track, not more than five or six hours old. The depth of the heel and the shape of the sole were typical of Mexican-style boots. Casting around, he discovered more. Six riders had briefly stopped at that very spot, then crossed.

"What is it?" the Kid inquired. Inspecting the tracks, he grew somber. "So. We have done what no one else could. My compliments. But what now?"

"We make camp."

"Right this moment? With so much daylight left?"

The site was ideal. Thick pines flanked the crescent-moon clearing. On the other side of the stream, however, the land was open. Infrequent boulders and patches of brush broke the monotony, few within reliable rifle range. At the end of the tableland, a mile off, stone cliffs towered to the sky. From up there a man could see forever. Which had probably induced El Gato to select it for his stronghold.

Fargo gathered wood for a fire. Enough for five fires, in fact, a huge mound that rose to his waist. The Kid helped, regarding him as if he were loco. The horses were tethered where they could get at grass and the water. Fargo insisted on bringing two logs and assorted boulders into the clearing and arranging them along the bank. They were to act as a barrier against stray lead.

Taking his rope, Fargo rigged a nasty surprise for anyone who tried to sneak up on them from the rear. He looped the rope from tree to tree at the height a man's chest would be when on horseback. The Durango Kid caught on right away and did the same with his own lariat. They left a gap only they would know about, just in case things went wrong.

The rest of the afternoon was spent collecting long, straight limbs and sharpening the thinner ends of each. The blunt ends were embedded in the ground and propped at a slant so that anyone who blundered into one would be impaled.

As the Kid trimmed tiny offshoots from one of the limbs, he winked at Fargo and said, "You have a devious mind, *compañero*. I am glad El Gato is not as smart as you."

Only one incident of note occurred. About four, as they were forming the large ring of stones in which the fire would be built, the scenic tranquillity of the San Juans was shattered by gunfire. At first there were scattered shots, then a ragged volley followed by more random blasts. Echoes rumbled off the upper slopes, distorting the sound. Fargo pegged the direction as southwest, but he could not estimate the distance accurately.

"What was that all about, you reckon?" the Durango Kid said. "The *banditos* found some new victims?"

"Way up here?" Fargo was mystified. No one else other than El Gato's band had a reason for being in the vicinity. Unless the Utes were involved. This was their territory, and they protected it fiercely. The justice of having the bandits wiped out by a war party appealed to him.

"Should we go have a look-see, *amigo*?" Alonzo asked.

"No." Fargo preferred to sit tight. Wandering off invited disaster. El Gato might spot them and cut them off before they could get back. All the labor that had gone into their trap would be for naught. "We'll stick to my plan."

"Ah, yes. Your plan. When do you suppose you can share it with me? After all, if I am to be the bait, it would be nice to know the part you expect me to play. Or will you simply stake me out and build a bonfire to attract Joaquin Hernandez?"

Fargo grinned. "How did you guess?"

By twilight they were set. The Kid was none too happy about the setup, but he confined his complaints to comments issued under his breath. Fargo waited until stars filled the sky to ignite the wood. He had to leap back when the large pile caught, the flames flaring four to five feet. The gusty wind helped immensely.

"I bet they can see that clear down in Animas City," the Kid quipped.

That was the general idea. Fargo counted on El Gato spying the fire from up on the heights. Curiosity would do the rest. He added a few limbs, then squatted to polish off more black coffee. Alonzo de Leon was scrutinizing him as if he were an animal Alonzo had never encountered.

"The odds against us are formidable. You know that, don't you?" The Kid threw a twig into the bonfire. "What is to keep me from leaving you to fend for yourself? If El Gato feeds your body to the scavengers, so much the better. No one will ever know."

"You will."

"You credit me with more morals than I have, Americano. I do not always do the right thing, as my stay in Durango proved." The Kid jerked back when a green branch exploded, showering him with sparks. "I am ashamed to admit that not everyone I killed was as deserving as Ignacio."

"I'll take my chances," Fargo said. "The trump card is in my favor."

"Clarice, you mean?" The Kid spun a rowel on a spur to hear it jingle. "We men do funny things when we fall in love, yes? We dream of them night and day. We miss them whenever they are away. And we are willing to make any sacrifice to please them. Even to go so far as to put our lives in jeopardy. Pathetic, eh?"

A hiss of burning wood and a loud crackle punctuated Alonzo's assessment. Fargo gazed toward the inky battlements that crowned the Divide. Tomorrow would be the test. If the outlaws saw the fire, they would lose no time in venturing down to investigate. The crucial question was how many would come? All of them, including El Gato? Or just a few to scout out the situation and report back?

Sleep was difficult to attain. Fargo dozed off often, but every noise, no matter how slight, brought him fully awake. And there were a lot—twigs snapping, leaves rustling, howls and yips and snarls. The mountains were alive with wildlife. Nighttime was the domain of the predators. Wolves and coyotes, bears and wolverines, the big cats and their lesser kin, all were abroad. Mingled with their cries were the squeals, screams, and screeches of their prey. It was not like down on the lowland where the mooing of cattle and the barking of dogs were the norm.

Fargo was up well before dawn. He had coffee brewing and was saddling the Ovaro when the Durango Kid sat up and blinked at the world in mild confusion.

"Where am I? Oh. Now I remember. I am where any man with common sense would not be. Today I sacrifice myself on the altar of love."

In all his travels Fargo had met few people with Alonzo's gift for flowery speech. Chuckling, he responded, "You're right where you have to be, so quit grousing. It's either this, or lose Clarice."

"Don't remind me. She has made a simpleton of me." The Kid yawned and stretched. "It makes me wonder. Twenty years from now will I be one of those married men who are led around on a leash by their wives? You know the kind. Men who have been castrated above the waist rather than below." He tossed his blanket off. "I tell you, *mi compañero*. This life is most baffling. It is best not to dwell on it too much, or you will start talking to yourself."

A golden glow spread across the land as the sun climbed the heavens. Fargo rekindled the bonfire, throwing clumps of wet weeds and grass on top to produce a dense column of spiraling smoke, a beacon to bring their adversaries. They rolled up their bedrolls and hid their mounts in the trees. The Kid carried his rifle to a log bordering the stream. Taking a seat, he inserted a sixth cartridge into his pistol. "Let us hope they don't keep us waiting long, eh?"

Nodding, Fargo went in among the pines. Picking one with a broad trunk and low-hanging limbs, he hunkered. Through a gap in the limbs he could see regal peaks glistening white with snow. Above them soared a golden eagle. Propping himself against the bole, he laid the Henry across his lap.

The morning crawled by. Twice Alonzo had to add wood to the bonfire. Four times he added soaked vegetation to create thicker smoke.

Fargo was inclined to think they were wasting their time when hooves drummed to the northeast—many hooves, raising a cloud of dust that partially obscured the mounts and the men riding them. He spread out flat and tucked the Henry to his shoulder. The sparkle of silver on saddles and several obvious sombreros relieved any worry he had that they were Utes and not the bandits.

El Gato had taken the bait. Fargo counted at least twelve *pistoleros*, but there might be more. He saw the Kid glance back at him as if to say, "See? You *are* insane." Then Alonzo calmly faced front to await their visitors.

The outlaws did not slow until they were a couple of hundred yards out. At a command from a husky man in the middle, they spread out in a skirmish line, just as a troop of cavalry would do. They were very disciplined, these *banditos*. Which increased the threat they posed. Two riders spurred ahead, galloping in close to the other side of the stream. They did not seem to recognize the Kid, either due to the fact he was wearing Varga's sombrero or because not all of El Gato's band had ever seen him. Alonzo smiled and waved.

The pair returned to the main body. A short consultation resulted in six of the band trotting forward in a compact group.

The Durango Kid shifted. "Do you see that ugly one in the center? The one with the crooked nose? You have gotten your wish, my friend. You are about to make El Gato's acquaintance."

7

The bandits slowly advanced to the opposite bank. El Gato constantly glanced to the right and the left, a swarthy hand resting on one of the twin pistols belted at his waist. He was suspicious, as well he should be. The outlaw had not survived as long as he had by taking anything for granted. When he reined up, so did the others, forming a partial ring around him.

Skye Fargo was trying to fix a bead on the butcher. But as luck would have it, one or another of the *pistoleros* was always in the way. When they stopped, a clear shot presented itself at last. He lined up the sights squarely on El Gato's chest, only to be foiled when a gunman's horse pranced sideways. All he could see of The Cat was a shoulder and arm.

The Durango Kid, meanwhile, sat with his head bowed, the sombrero hiding his features. He idly pried at the log, whistling softly as if he did not have a care in the world. He continued to whistle even after the *banditos* stopped. They did not know what to make of his antics and glanced at one another.

In Spanish, El Gato called out, "Hello there, friend. Who are you? Are you lost, that you have strayed so far into the wilderness?"

Some of the gunmen snickered. The Kid did not look up. He answered huskily, disguising his voice. "I am right where I need to be," he quoted Fargo. "What about you, *señor*? Are you and your companions lost? Or do you live out here with the Indians?"

Fargo started to slide to the right to get a clear shot. He

had to move slowly in order not to be detected. Out on the tableland the remaining bandits were waiting for a signal from their boss. The dust had settled, showing that there were twelve, all told, after all.

"I am Joaquin Hernandez," The Cat was saying. "Perhaps you have heard of me? Men call me El Gato."

"What an odd name," the Kid said. "Is it because you have the reflexes of a cat? Or are you covered with fur and have a tail?"

Some of the *pistoleros* laughed. El Gato was not one of them. "I was given my nickname because I am as vicious as a Durango alley cat. It would not do to anger me, stranger. Just ask any of the dozens of *hombres* I have buried."

"Only *hombres*?" the Kid responded. "I have heard that you kill women and children, as well. That you have left a bloody trail from Mexico to this territory. That in all the world, no *bandito* can rival the famous El Gato."

Was it an insult or a compliment? That was the question Hernandez could not seem to decide. He tugged at his long mustache, pondering.

Fargo could now see more of The Cat, but not enough to guarantee that a single shot would do the job. Another foot to the right, and the Kid himself was in the line of fire. His plan had gone awry. To shoot El Gato he must crawl into the open, and the moment he did, all hell would break loose.

"So you do know who I am, stranger," El Gato hollered. "I think you came here just to see me. That is why you made your fire so big last night. That is why you made so much smoke today."

"Nothing gets past you, does it?" the Kid said. "*Sí.* I came to find you, famous one. I have heard that you are always open to accepting new men. Men who can kill without qualms. Men who are fast with a gun."

"You want to join my band?" El Gato said, flattered. "Why didn't you just come out and say so? Who are you? Somehow, you are familiar to me."

"Maybe it is this hat," the Kid said, tapping the sombrero. "It belonged to someone who was a close friend of yours. Varga."

The Cat and the men with him stiffened. El Gato scanned the clearing, lingering on the logs that had been placed near the stream. He scanned it again, and his head snapped back. "Where is your horse? And your gear? Did you fly here? Or crawl on your belly like the miserable snake that you are, de Leon?"

The Kid slowly lifted his head, smiling broadly. "So you recognized me finally, eh? I have come to end this thing between us, Joaquin. Sending Varga and those others to gun me down was a mistake. It made me realize that the only way to stop you was to confront you personally." The Kid stood. "I challenge you, Joaquin Hernandez, here and now, in front of your men. Prove to them you are not a coward. Show them you do not need others to do what you should do yourself."

El Gato did not like it one bit. He went to reply, then noticed that the *pistoleros* were all staring at him. Gnawing on his lower lip, he stalled.

"What is the matter?" the Kid bated him. "Can it be that you are afraid to meet me man to man? Varga was brave enough to do it. So were Pedro, Ramon, and Lopez. Of course, their stupidity got them killed. But that is beside the point. Will you, or will you not, do what you ordered them to do? Put an end to your hatred, one way or the other."

El Gato was as sly as he was bloodthirsty. "How do I know you came alone?" he countered. "How do I know that others are not hidden in those trees?"

Raising his voice, the Durango Kid said, "I give you my solemn word that no one will interfere if you climb down and face me."

The outcome hung in the balance. Fargo had crawled far enough to the right to have a clear shot at El Gato's head, but he held his fire. He would honor the Kid's request, although he doubted that The Cat would. Hernandez was no fool. The bandit knew he was no match for the Kid. El Gato would come up with some excuse to back out.

At that juncture fickle fate played a hand. Back in the trees, one of the horses whinnied.

El Gato seized the moment. "Did you hear that?" he bawled to his men. "It is a trap! Kill him! Kill them all!" Out swept his pistol.

The Kid was faster. His own revolver appeared out of thin air, leveled at Hernandez. But at the very split second his finger tightened on the trigger, one of the bandits came between them. The slug meant for El Gato tore through the *pistolero*. And then all the bandits were firing, forcing the Kid to drop behind the log.

Fargo added the Henry to the fray. His first shot nailed a man unlimbering a rifle. The smoke from the Henry gave his position away, and in another moment slugs were ripping through the pine above and plowing into the earth on either side.

"Back, *amigos!* Back!" El Gato shouted, leading his cutthroats in a rush to get out of range.

A hundred yards out, the other six were charging to their leader's rescue. Rifles and pistols blazing, they peppered the camp. Most of their fire was concentrated on the log protecting the Kid.

Fargo heaved out from under the tree. He dropped an onrushing rider, the gunman spilling from the saddle like a disjointed doll. Hornets buzzed past as he zigzagged toward the logs, firing on the fly. It was at moments like this he most appreciated the Henry. His old rifle, a Sharps, had held a single cartridge at a time. The Henry held fifteen rounds in a tubular magazine under the barrel. No other rifle could boast the same capacity. In the hands of a marksman, it was devastating.

His blistering fire turned the charging bandits. Veering away, they joined El Gato and the rest in flight. When they were safely out of range, they slowed. A few shouted oaths and shook fists. Presently, they disappeared in the distance.

The Durango Kid was fit to be tied. Rising, he angrily threw the sombrero to the ground and stomped in a circle like a bull gone amok. "Damn our luck!" he declared. "I had him! Had him right where I wanted him! If not for that fool horse, Hernandez would be dead!"

Fargo put a foot on a log and began replacing the bullets he had expended. "It's not over yet. They'll be back."

"What makes you so sure?"

"El Gato is not about to let an opportunity like this slip by. Now he knows there are only two of us. He'll try to overwhelm us by sheer numbers. As soon as they regroup, they'll hit us from all different directions."

"Good. Let them." The Kid retrieved the sombrero and slapped it against his leg to remove dust. "I meant what I said about ending this one way or another. I am not leaving these mountains until I spit in Joaquin's lifeless face."

"Take off your hat and jacket," Fargo said.

"What for?"

"You'll see."

Fargo had a hunch they did not have much time. El Gato probably expected them to light a shuck for Animas City now that their trap had failed, and he would be eager to prevent them from escaping. Little did The Cat realize that they had no intention of leaving until they had done what they set out to do. Dashing to the pile of unused firewood, he selected several branches over four feet long. Propping two of them against one another behind the log that had shielded the Kid during the gun battle, he draped the Kid's jacket over them and added the sombrero as a crowning touch.

Alonzo laughed. "No one would mistake that for a real person. They will see through your ruse."

"Not until they're close," Fargo said. "By the time they do, we'll have them in our gun sights."

Propping a second pair of makeshift poles beside a boulder, Fargo topped them with his own hat, stripped off his buckskin shirt, and tied the shirt around them. "From a distance, it will do."

At that altitude the air was brisk. Fargo turned to fetch his spare shirt from his saddlebags. A glimmer of sunlight off metal brought him up short. Screening his eyes with a hand, he saw a knot of riders looping around their position well beyond rifle range. "They're already at it," he announced, pointing. "That bunch will cut us off from the rear."

"And there are more," the Kid said.

To the southeast a second bunch was hastening across the tableland. Fargo counted four men, all armed with rifles. "Get under cover," he said, dashing into the trees. He found a suitable spot, a cluster of firs. From there he could see the stream, on one hand, and part of the rope they had strung, on the other. The Kid went to ground twenty feet to the west in a clump of brush.

A hush gripped the tableland. The birds had fallen silent. Other animals were lying low in their dens or burrows. Not so much as a chipmunk stirred. Was it due to the gunfire a short while ago, or did the animals somehow sense that violence was about to erupt again? Fargo could not say. Wild creatures demonstrated an uncanny knack in that regard.

To the north a horse nickered. To the south hooves pounded. To the east rose a muted rumbling. The *banditos* were closing in. Confident in their superior numbers, they would strike hard and fast. Fargo could only hope that the surprises he had arranged would slow them down some, allowing the Kid and him to pick their targets. He saw four men approaching from the northeast. Among them was El Gato. Whooping and waving their rifles, the quartet spread out, bearing down on the dummy figures. Seconds later, to the southeast, more *pistoleros* appeared. They were coordinating their attack so that all three groups struck at the same time.

The third bunch! Fargo spun, hearing branches crack and brush crackle. The men who had circled to the north were coming through the trees. He glimpsed a splash of color, a man's shirt and pants. The Durango Kid's rifle boomed, to be answered by several shots in unison. Fargo snapped lead at a gunman who promptly melted into the growth. Slugs started to zip past from several directions. The gunmen to the northeast and those to the southeast had taken the initial shots as their cue to open fire in earnest. A withering firestorm poured into the clearing and the pines. Pivoting, he aimed at the foremost rider to the southeast and brought the killer crashing to earth.

To the northeast El Gato and the men with him concentrated their fire on the dummy figures. Suddenly, the one Fargo had set up to resemble the Kid tilted wildly and fell, collapsing in on itself. El Gato yelled instructions Fargo could not hear. Immediately, The Cat and the others angled toward the trees, intending to cross the stream above the logs and boulders.

Fargo barreled through the woods to intercept them. He came to a patch of clear ground and saw one of the bandits plunge into the water, spray flying from under the horse. The man saw Fargo almost at the same instant and extended a Sharps. Fargo put two shots into him before he could get off one. Upended, the *pistolero* tumbled into the stream.

Behind Fargo a flurry of gunshots testified to the Kid's stiff resistance. An outlaw was cursing vilely. From the area where Fargo had erected the sharpened poles, a man screamed in torment.

Darting behind a tree, Fargo sank onto a knee and steadied the Henry. El Gato and two others were almost across, all three firing into the vegetation with reckless abandon. They had lost track of him. Quickly, Fargo centered the rifle on The Cat. Unfortunately, El Gato spurred in among some pines and was lost to view.

From the clearing rose the driving beat of hooves. The group from the southeast had arrived. Fargo shifted to hold them at bay and saw the Kid already dealing with the situation. Bursting from cover, the Kid whipped out his ivory-handled Colt and fired three times from the hip. A *bandito* was jarred by a slug, but stayed in the saddle. Another wrenched to one side, blood spurting from a shoulder.

A hail of lead drove the Kid back. He sought cover with dirt kicking up at his heels. Out of the trees to his left loomed another rider, a rifle leveled. Fargo banged off a shot a fraction ahead of Alonzo. Whether they scored or not was hard to tell, but the rider did rein off and was swallowed by evergreens.

Someone roared orders in Spanish. The rending of limbs to Fargo's right brought him around in a crouch. But none of their enemies were visible. Hooves drummed, receding, not growing louder. It was the same to the north and south. Belatedly, he realized the bandits had taken enough. El Gato had called off the attack.

Warily, Fargo moved toward the Kid. Groans to his right drew him to an outlaw who had been impaled by one of the sharpened poles. Like a pig on a spit, the bandit hung a foot off the ground, arms and legs thrashing feebly. The oversized spear had sheared into his abdomen and out his back. His pants and the grass underneath were soaked red. Weakly, he raised his arms to push against the pole. To no avail. Nothing humanly possible could be done for him. The suffering he endured contorted his face.

Fargo shot him, once, through the temple. Going on, he discovered where an outlaw had ridden into the rope he had stretched between trees. The rope had snapped and lay in a tangle. Footprints showed where the man had risen and stumbled to a horse.

"*Amigo?*"

The Kid was in the clearing. Fargo jogged over, passing a gunman whose left eye oozed gore. "Were you hit?"

"No. You?"

Fargo shook his head. To the east the bandits were regrouping. Eight, he counted, three of whom were slumped over, evidently wounded. "We drove them off," he said, not quite able to believe they had accomplished it.

"Yes. But Joaquin got away." The Kid swore luridly. "He has the nine lives of his namesake, that one. What do we do next? I do not think he will be rash enough to try that again."

Nor did Fargo. A third of the band had died, maybe another third was hurting. El Gato would not stick around now that he had lost the advantage. "Mount up. We're going after them."

"Now you are talking!" the Kid declared.

They reclaimed their clothing and raced to their horses. Fargo took a few moments to gather up his rope but the Kid did not bother with the lariat. Impatient to be off, he kept saying, "Hurry, *compañero*. Hurry."

At a trot they crossed the clearing, vaulted the logs, and forded the stream. To the south a cloud of dust marked El Gato's flight. Fargo gave the stallion its head and rapidly pulled away from the Kid's sorrel. He had traveled a quarter of a mile when he was startled to see a lone *pistolero* ahead, on foot. The gunman was propped against a boulder, aiming a rifle. Fargo reined to one side just as the rifle spouted smoke and lead. Yanking out his Colt, Fargo headed straight for the rifleman, who was awkwardly reloading. At a hundred yards he fired once and missed, knowing he would, but wanting to rattle the bandit. At seventy-five yards he chipped slivers from the boulder, a remarkable shot for someone moving at a full gallop. At fifty yards he held his arm as steady as he could and squeezed the trigger simultaneously with the outlaw. He thought to wing the killer, but the man sank down where he stood, and if not for the boulder would have keeled backward.

Stricken, yet alive, the gunman plucked at a pistol. He was too weak to draw and gave up with a sigh.

Fargo slowed. A crimson stain high on the man's chest marked where his slug had hit. Another, larger, stain covered the midsection. Fargo had wondered what the man hoped to achieve by standing up to them. Now he knew. The *bandito* had been severely wounded during the gunfight at their camp, too severely to go much farther. So the man opted to be left behind, to go down fighting rather than bleed to death.

The Kid galloped up. He took one look at the bandit and put two slugs into his chest. "What are you waiting for?" he said, and hastened on without a backward glance.

Fargo followed. Soon he took the lead again thanks to the pinto's superb stamina. The dust cloud expanded. In due course dark figures were apparent. At the grueling pace the bandits had set, Fargo figured they would ride their steeds into the ground before nightfall. He slowed just enough to keep them in sight and not overtire the Ovaro.

For the next half an hour the pursuit continued. Fargo did not lose any ground, but the Kid did, falling farther behind every mile. Still, Fargo figured on overtaking The Cat soon. A yell from the Durango Kid changed everything. Alonzo had slowed to a walk. The sorrel was limping, and limping badly.

The chase had to be suspended. Burning with annoyance, Fargo rode back. A swollen leg explained what had happened. The Kid was examining it, frowning.

"Of all the cursed luck! This animal will be next to useless for four or five days. Let me borrow your pinto. You can camp here until I am done with Hernandez."

"We'll ride double." Fargo seldom let anyone else ride the Ovaro, even friends of long acquaintance. He had only let Clarice and Lucas do so because the old-timer was gravely hurt. But some who might say it was silly to be so fussy had never depended on a horse for their very survival. Bending, he beckoned. "Leave it. Bring just your rifle."

The delay cost them dearly. Now the bandits had a commanding lead. The dust cloud had dwindled, nearing forested slopes crowned by lofty summits. Once the outlaws gained the heavy timber, flushing them out would be difficult.

Despite the setback, Fargo held the Ovaro to a trot. For him to push harder ran the risk of the pinto going lame. Rising in the stirrups every so often, he tracked the bandits as they climbed a slope to a bench and from there entered growth so thick that he could not pinpoint which way they had gone.

"They seek high ground," the Kid said. "They will hide up there and pick us off at their leisure."

"Not if I can help it," Fargo stated. He had survived encounters with Apaches and Comanches, and the bandits could not be any more shrewd than the warriors of the wastelands.

"When next we tangle with them, I crave a favor." The Kid did not say what it was, but Fargo could guess.

"You want El Gato for yourself?"

"*Sí, por favor*. He must pay for the suffering he has

caused Clarice, for the torment he brought to my father and mother. If anyone has a right to end his life, I do." The Kid patted his pistol. "He will die slowly, a bullet at a time."

"As much as I would like to give my word, I can't make any promises," Fargo said. He elaborated. "El Gato is just as liable to throw down on me as he is on you. I can hardly ask him to hold his fire until you have a free moment."

"Understood. Even so, if you are able, save the pig for me. I will be eternally in your debt."

The tableland ended at the bottom of the steep slope. Fargo had the Kid dismount and did likewise. On foot they ascended to the bench. The woodland beyond lay serene under the afternoon sun. Handing the reins to Alonzo, Fargo sprinted into the trees. Tracks revealed that El Gato had pressed on, to the southeast. Signaling the Kid to bring the stallion, Fargo resumed the manhunt. Logs and boulders and varied obstacles slowed them down considerably. So much so, that by late afternoon they were four or five miles behind their quarry. Fargo hated to admit it, but El Gato was on the verge of slipping through their fingers.

The Kid fell into one of his sulks. As glum as a rainy day, he protested when Fargo called a halt with an hour of daylight remaining. "We cannot afford to waste a minute. Ride on until midnight, then start again two hours before sunrise. It is our only hope."

"No," Fargo refused to ruin the stallion. "My horse needs rest. The best we can do is dog El Gato's trail until he makes a mistake or our luck changes."

Disgusted, Alonzo slid down and did not utter another word until nine that night. A small fire warmed them. Fargo gave one of his blankets to the Kid and received a curt "*Gracias.*" Squatting and treating himself to his third cup of coffee, Fargo contemplated their prospects. Were they fooling themselves? he wondered. Realistically, what chance did they have of catching The Cat with one mount between them?

The Durango Kid turned, the blanket draped over his shoulders. "I am sorry for how I have acted today," he said. "I have been childish." When Fargo did not comment, he said, "Hatred eats at a man like termites eat wood. It warps our minds, makes us do things we would never do otherwise."

From the peaks above wafted the howl of a lonesome wolf. The Kid peered at the inky crags and grew sad. "I know how *el lobo* feels. My heart hurts, I miss Clarice so much." He rose to pour coffee. "How about you, my friend? Have you ever been struck by lighting, as they say in Mexico? Have you ever been so in love that you could not bear to be away from the woman of your dreams for more than a minute?"

"No."

The Kid looked at him askance. "Oh, come now. Surely you have been smitten by Cupid's arrows once or twice?"

"Not in the way you mean."

Digesting this, the Kid sat back down. "Then I am sorry for you, Skye Fargo. To live a life without love is to live an empty existence. As the tutor my father hired to instruct me in classic literature was so fond of saying, *amor vincit omnia*. Your day will come."

Alonzo de Leon was a bundle of surprises. The more Fargo learned, the more amazed he was that Alonzo had left the *hacienda* for a life of wine, women, and song. A man like his father, Manuel, a man who spared no expense in the raising of his son, was the sort of man any boy would be proud to call father.

"Can I confide a secret?" the Kid asked, and did not wait for an answer. "When I was younger, I courted the notion of one day being a great poet. Can you imagine? Me? Writing romantic verse?"

Fargo could readily imagine it, but he spared the Kid the indignity of saying so. Abruptly, in the woods to the southeast, twigs cracked, brush snapped. Something big was approaching. Fargo palmed the Colt and glided to a boulder. The Kid ducked behind a tree. As high-strung as they were, it was a credit to their self-control that they did not shoot when an animal blundered into their camp.

"*Madre de Dios!*" the Kid exclaimed.

An oath escaped Fargo, too. What he was seeing simply

could not be. They were many miles from the lowland valleys, three full days from Animas City. No one they knew should be there, certainly not the owner of the horse that pawed the ground and bobbed its weary head.

It was a zebra dun. *Wanda's* zebra dun.

8

No two horses were ever exactly alike. No two pintos or paints had the same markings, no two Appaloosas the same spots, no two zebra duns had the same markings. An experienced horseman could always tell one from another. Wanda's dun not only had a stripe the entire length of its top line, but stripes on its legs, as well. In this instance, added proof that it was her animal were the saddlebags; she had stitched her initials into the flaps.

Speaking softly so as not to spook it, Fargo walked toward the dangling reins. "There, there, big fella," he said. "Everything is fine now. Stand still." He rambled on, the dun eyeing him with ears pricked. Once he took hold of the bridle, he stroked its neck and patted its sides, calming it down. Sweat lathered the coat. Burrs were stuck to the legs, mane, and tail—evidence the horse had been wandering on its own for quite some time.

The Durango Kid had the good sense not to come over until the animal stood docile and at ease. "It's Wanda's, isn't it?" he asked. When Fargo nodded, he placed a hand on its neck. "How can this be, *amigo?* Do you think it followed us into the mountains on its own?"

"Not very likely," Fargo said, not with the saddle on, plus a bedroll and a sack that hung from the horn. Opening the latter, he rummaged through enough supplies to last a couple of weeks. It allowed for only one conclusion, incredible as it seemed. For some inexplicable reason, Wanda had ridden into the high country on her own. She had trailed them, and something had happened to her. He recollected the shots they had heard the day before, and worry gnawed at him like a beaver gnawing at wood.

The Kid was just as bewildered. "It makes no sense. Why would she be so foolish? You told her to stay in town where it was safe." A thought struck him, and he paled. "Sweet Mary! What if she brought Clarice along?"

"We'll backtrack the dun in the morning," Fargo said. The Kid looked at him, and they both knew what the other was thinking. If they turned aside to find Wanda, they lost any slim chance they had left of catching up to El Gato.

"How could things go so wrong?" Alonzo lamented. "We almost had him! All it would have taken was one shot! And now . . . !" In baffled impotence he smacked a fist against an open palm. "Now we must start all over again. Only it will be much harder. He will not fall for our tricks a second time."

Fargo was concerned that The Cat would quit the territory, maybe venture south of the border for a spell to lick his wounds and rebuild his band. It might be months before El Gato showed up again, and by then Fargo would be long gone. The people of Animas City would be no better off than they had been when he rode into their valley.

Unsaddling the dun, Fargo tethered it near the Ovaro. The exhausted animal nipped at grass, but did not eat much. It was asleep within ten minutes.

For Fargo and the Kid, sleep was more elusive. Fargo tossed and turned, dozing in snatches, awakening with a start more times than he cared to count. Worry for Wanda was only partly to blame. He couldn't shake a nagging feeling of unease. Whether it had to do with El Gato or the dun or something else was a mystery. By morning he was cramped and stiff and felt as if he needed a solid ten hour's sleep. In the predawn darkness he set coffee to boiling and made do with pemmican for breakfast. He let the Kid rest until it was almost time to head out.

Backtracking was a challenge. The ground was rocky and hard, and the dun had meandered erratically. By noon they had gone only six miles. At one point the trail suggested that the dun had started down toward the lowland, only to reverse itself and stray into the timber. By two in the afternoon they were southeast of their original camp site. In a clearing Fargo found where the dun and another horse had halted. The prints were obvious even to someone who was not a tracker, like the Kid.

Alonzo groaned. "Clarice. It must be. They came together. But what in God's name were they trying to prove?"

Fargo circled the clearing. The tracks led in at a walk and departed at a gallop. He learned why when he came on another set of tracks, hoofprints of ten or eleven horses that raced out of the trees to the southwest. Wanda and the other rider had fled for their lives.

The new development rattled the Kid. "It must have been some of El Gato's band. He has more men than we thought."

Fargo wished that were the case. Pointing at the churned earth, he said, "I'm afraid not. Those horses weren't shod."

"They were not wearing shoes?" Alonzo said. It was several seconds before the implication jarred him. "Indians! But the only tribe in these parts are the Utes, and they are not friendly to whites."

No, they were not, Fargo mused. But the Utes had not killed anyone, yet. Nor had there been any reports of females being abducted. The Utes were not like the Comanches, who had a history of kidnapping white women.

Tracks told the whole story. For the better part of four miles the chase had gone on. Wanda and the other rider had flung lead at the Indians to keep them at bay. Then the other rider's horse had stumbled and thrown the rider. In swooped the warriors, who overpowered Wanda and her companion. In the confusion, the zebra dun had bolted. Several warriors went after it, but it eluded them.

Dismounting, Fargo examined individual tracks closely. Since no two tribes crafted their moccasins in the same manner, frontiersmen worthy of the name could tell one from the other by the little differences, the shapes of the soles, the style of stitching, and so on. These were definitely Ute prints. As for Wanda's companion, the outline of the shoes, the narrow soles and small heels, confirmed it had been a woman.

The Kid was anxious to be off. "We must hurry and save them. If the Indians take them deep into the mountains, no one will ever see them again."

For the rest of the day and into the evening they rode hard, making good time now that both of them had a mount again. Fargo mentioned Alonzo's own animal, but the Kid could not be bothered. "I will go get it after Clarice is safe in my arms, and not before."

The Utes had done as Alonzo feared and headed into the heart of the San Juans. The next day was spent climbing, always climbing, to a cold pass so high up, they had the illusion of being on top of the world. Fargo drew rein to give the stallion a breather and surveyed the vast expanse of country below. The view was breathtaking. Another time, another place, he would have lingered to enjoy it. Not today. At the Kid's prodding they crossed the Divide and descended into virgin wilderness, a hunter's paradise rife with game, the exclusive domain of the Utes.

Fargo was on his guard every second. Hunting parties would be abroad. War parties were bound to be coming and going. He kept the Henry across the saddle, a cartridge in the chamber. A series of switchbacks brought them to a bluff overlooking what the old-timers called a "park," a high valley lush with grass and water. From trees beside a small lake tendrils of smoke curled skyward.

"We've found them!" the Kid cried.

"Yell a little louder, why don't you?" Fargo said irritably. "They might not have heard you."

"Sorry, my friend." The Kid flourished his pistol and spun it on a finger. "Now we go down there, eh? And wipe the red devils out."

"I'm going down. You're staying here." Fargo did not want the hothead with him when he attempted a rescue. It would be like trying to put out a fire by throwing another match on the flames. "And we're not shooting anyone if we can help it." The Kid started to object, but Fargo gestured sharply. "This land belongs to the Utes. It's their home.

They have every right to deal with outsiders as they see fit. So long as they haven't harmed the women, we're not harming them. Savvy?"

"You surprise me, Skye. Most white men believe that the only good Indian is a dead Indian."

"Just because most people believe something doesn't make it right." Fargo lifted the reins, then paused. "By the way. Thanks."

"For what?"

"Calling me by my name. If you had called me *amigo* one more time, I was liable to shoot you."

Descending to the valley floor took some doing. Fargo was halfway down the bluff when a party of six warriors appeared. They were riding in single file, from north to south, toward the lake. He was so intent on the area around it that he did not see the newcomers until it was almost too late. Cutting into some aspens, he reined up and raised the Henry. No outcry rang out, though. The newcomers had not spotted him.

The six Utes led a horse laden with the body of a buck. None were painted for war, which was encouraging. They filed along the west shoreline, to be greeted by friendly shouts. From out of the trees came four warriors. A brief palavar was held, after which the whole group went into the pines.

Fargo let fifteen minutes go by before he nudged the stallion. No other Indians had shown, so he deemed it safe enough. The column of smoke had grown thicker and darker, a sign the Utes were building up their fire in preparation for a feast.

A thicket offered a convenient hiding place for the pinto. Moving to the treeline, he pondered how to reach the lake without being spotted. There was absolutely no cover, other than the grass, which was knee-high. Lowering onto his hands and knees, he crawled. Here and there the grass thinned, forcing him to take a roundabout course. He was sixty yards out when three warriors rode out of the copse directly at him.

Thinking he had been seen, Fargo flattened and sighted

on the foremost rider. But the Utes were talking and joking, not notching arrows or hefting lances. Sitting proud and straight, they had no inkling there was a white man within fifty miles. Soon they would, however, if he stayed where he was. Crawling to the left into the thickest grass he could find, Fargo waited with held breath for the warriors to go by.

The Utes were a handsome people. The men had clean complexions, oval faces, and wide nostrils. These were dressed in buckskins adorned with beadwork. Two of the men wore single feathers in their long braided hair. They were armed with the type of small bow favored by the tribe, a weapon that for centuries had served them in good stead. For untold centuries the tribe had held their mountain fastness against all enemies, until the coming of the whites and firearms put their way of life in jeopardy.

Fargo guessed they were from the Yampa branch of the tribe, a powerful band that had successfully contended with the Kiowas and Arapahos, among others. One by one the riders went past, so close that he could have tossed a stone and hit one. He had an apprehensive moment when the middle horse flared its nostrils and whinnied, as if it had caught his scent. But the warrior riding it slapped his legs against its sides and rode on.

As soon as they were gone, Fargo hastened eastward. A winding gully not apparent from the bluff afforded him an avenue of reaching the lake unseen. It came out forty yards south of the encampment. From its rim he saw racks of elk and deer meat drying in the sun. Temporary conical lodges had been erected, enough to house over twenty warriors. Only thirteen were present, but that was still thirteen too many. Two of them were sharpening knives. Others were making arrows. Still others were playing a game with bone dice.

Five Ute women were there, too. A couple of young ones were butchering the elk. Another pair was busy skinning a recently slain elk. The fifth was by the fire, pouring broth into a bowl. Fargo focused on her. Filling it, she walked to a pole lodge and bent to go in. When she came back out a minute later, she did not have the bowl with her. Was that where Wanda and Clarice were? he speculated.

The Utes did not have their horses in a string, as whites would do. Each warrior tied his mount close to the lodge in which he slept, enabling Fargo to tell which lodges were being used and which were not. One of those nearest him appeared to be unoccupied. He kept it in mind for later.

The time passed uneventfully. Having butchered the buck, the two women set to work roasting it. The elk was carved into thin slices, the meat hung over a rack to dry. From the look of things, the hunting party was laying up enough to last their people for months. As for the warriors playing dice, they finished their game and several of their number walked toward the lodge in which Fargo suspected the Howards had been placed. A tall warrior entered. Whatever occurred in there caused a shriek of outrage. Rapidly, the warrior backed out again, an arm protecting his eyes from the nails of the woman trying to rip them out.

Wanda Howard stood outside the lodge, furious. Her fingers clawed, she raked the Ute's face, opening a cheek. The warrior dodged another swing, then gripped her wrists. He did not twist them, or in any way seek to hurt her. Holding fast, he addressed her in his own tongue. Fargo did not know the Ute language, but he did not need to. It was as plain as the nose on his face that the warrior wanted her to simmer down. It was like asking a wet bobcat to stay calm.

"Let go of me, you damned heathen!" Wanda railed. "Ever lay a hand on either of us again, and I'll blind you. So help me."

Threats were only effective if the one being threatened understood the peril. Since the warrior did not know a word of English, he smiled, then uttered more remarks in Ute.

Not pacified one whit, Wanda jerked her arms from his grasp and blocked the opening. "I meant it, you polecat. We're not your playthings. Try to force your will on us and you'll rue the day you were born."

The Utes exchanged perplexed looks. An older warrior reached for Wanda's arm and had his fingers soundly slapped. Others laughed. They laughed harder when the older warrior mimicked Wanda's savage expression and her slap.

Wanda did not know when to leave well enough alone. "Are you poking fun at me, you mangy bastard?" she snarled. "There's not a lick of manners among the whole bunch. Give me my guns back and I'll teach you! By God, I'll give you a taste of what you deserve for taking us captive."

Ignoring her, the Utes dispersed. The Ute woman who had brought the broth now brought a bark plate heaped with deer meat. She held it out for Wanda to take, but Wanda lashed at her, tipping the bark and spilling the chunks. Upset, the woman retreated. Wanda beamed in triumph, then shook her fist. "That will show you! Let us go or leave us be!"

Fargo did not see where starving to death would accomplish much. It was smarter to eat whatever was offered to keep one's strength up for an escape attempt. He watched Wanda back into the lodge and heard a low voice, then weeping. Clarice, by the sound. Why on earth they had come to the high country, he could not imagine. They had a lot of explaining to do once he freed them.

Since there was nothing to be done until dark, Fargo propped his chin on his forearms and rested. The three Utes who had left earlier did not return by sunset. That was when the warriors and women gathered around a pair of small fires to eat their evening meal. No one bothered to take food to Wanda and Clarice—and Fargo didn't blame them. After supper, the Utes huddled to swap stories. The men, that is. The women retired to a lodge reserved for them.

Fargo waited patiently as one warrior after another turned in for the night. As always, a few stayed up much later than everyone else. The older warrior liked to tell tales, and two younger ones could not get enough of them. It was past midnight when the venerable Ute shuffled to his lodge. Several minutes more, and the others followed suit.

One of the fires had died out. The second had been allowed to taper to flickering flames. Most of the lodges were plunged in murky shadow. Not the one that contained the Howard girls, regrettably. Fargo chafed while marking time until the last of the flames fizzed into nothingness. Rising, he began to cat-foot into the open, only to halt when the crunch of a footstep warned him he was not alone.

Dodging behind a bush, Fargo scoured the encampment. None of the Utes had reappeared, and none of the horses were moving around. But at the edge of the trees a figure materialized, moving along the perimeter toward him. When the shape was close enough, he pounced, clamping an arm around the figure's throat and a hand over the mouth. "Not a peep, you jackass! It's me."

The Durango Kid ceased struggling. He did not resist as Fargo pulled him into the undergrowth.

"What the hell are you trying to do? Get us all killed?"

"I could not wait any longer," the Kid whispered. "I feared something had happened to you. So I snuck on down." Eagerly, he gazed at the conical lodges. "Are they here? Have you seen them?"

"Yes."

"Then what are we waiting for?"

Spiriting the women out of there would be hard enough, Fargo reflected, without the Kid to complicate matters. At handling a pistol the Kid was top-notch, but when it came to moving about stealthily, his skill left a lot to be desired. "Did you see my pinto on your way here?"

"Sure did. I left the dun with it."

"Go to them. Be ready to ride out at a moment's notice."

Alonzo stepped back. "You make a poor joke, eh? The woman I love is in danger. It is my duty to do what I can to save her." Facing the camp, he put a hand on his revolver. "Let the Utes do their worst. They will pay dearly."

Frowning, Fargo selected his next words carefully. Woodcraft was called for, not blazing Colts. Attempting to get the women out of there at gunpoint was bound to result in all of them being slain. "It was no joke," he insisted. "Unless the horses are ready, the Utes will overtake us. We won't get a mile." As extra incentive, Fargo mentioned,

"Someone has to cover us. Who better for the job than you?"

The Kid's brow furrowed. It was a while before he answered. "Sí. Don't worry. I will do as you want. But if I hear a shot, I will come to help." Touching the sombrero's brim, he hurried westward. Even though he had removed his spurs, he still made enough noise for a couple of horses to show some interest. They stared, but neither whinnied.

Venturing from concealment, Fargo strode toward the lodge. He did not run for fear the patter would rouse the warriors to arms. Most tribes lived in constant dread of being raided, and from an early age warriors were trained to leap to the defense of their loved ones at any hour of the day or night.

No one opposed him, no one challenged him. Had it been a village, and not a hunting camp, the situation would have been a lot different. Villages crawled with dogs and kids. A person could not go two feet without a mongrel sniffing at his heels.

A blanket had been hung over the opening. Rather than whisper their names and risk being overhead, Fargo barged on in. He figured they would be asleep, exhausted by their ordeal. It was even darker in the lodge than it had been outside, and it took a few moments for his eyes to adjust. He did not see the blow that slammed into his shins, but he certainly felt it. Knocked off his feet, he sprawled onto his stomach. As he opened his mouth to let them know who he was, a strip of cloth wrapped itself around his throat. Simultaneously, a knee jammed into his spine and someone hauled backward on the strip.

Fargo would not have believed it possible. In the span of five seconds, the sisters had him down and were strangling the life out of him. Hands grasped at his wrists to pin them. Tearing loose, he snatched at the cloth, but it would not yield. Sputtering, he tried to say his name, but only managed a choked gurgle.

"Harder, Sis, harder!" Clarice whispered. "Kill the heathen!"

Her fingers closed on Fargo's left wrist. Grabbing her

arm with his other hand, he pulled with all his might, jerking her off balance. She was thrown onto his back, colliding with Wanda. Briefly, the pressure on their crude garrote lessened. It was all Fargo needed. Surging onto his hands and knees, he flung himself backward, bucking Wanda off. She squawked, Clarice swore, and both rose to confront him. In the dark their faces were pale masks of pure rage. They were intent on killing him and escaping, or to be killed in turn.

As they moved toward him, Fargo snapped his name, adding, "If I'd known you were going to choke me to death, I'd have let you save yourselves."

"Skye!" Wanda exclaimed, throwing herself at him. Her arms wrapped around his chest, her lips smothered his. She lavished hot kisses on his cheeks and chin, bit his jaw. "I could eat you alive! How did you find us?"

"It's not important." Fargo headed for the blanket. "We have to get out of here before someone comes."

Wanda glanced at her sister. "We can't."

Fargo did not want to delay another instant. The ruckus they had made might spoil everything. "Why the hell not?" he demanded.

"It's my right leg," Clarice said. "My horse threw me when the Utes were after us. I don't think it's busted, but the ankle is swollen something awful. I can hobble around, but I can't run."

As the old saw went, if it wasn't one thing, it was another. Fargo hunkered and gingerly inspected her leg. The right ankle was twice the size of the left. "I'll carry you," he said, and went to lift her. To his chagrin, she pushed against his shoulders.

"Hold on. Where's Alonzo? Why isn't he with you?"

Precious seconds were being squandered. Fargo came close to throwing her over his shoulder and making a run for it. But knowing the sisters, Clarice would vent her spleen and awaken the whole damn camp. "The Kid is waiting with the horses. We'll have to ride double, but if we keep going all night, we should be safe by morning." He thought that would suffice and bent to pick her up.

"Just a minute. Don't you want to hear why we came after you?"

Exasperated to the limits of his endurance, Fargo toyed with the notion of slugging her. "Not *now*."

Wanda stepped closer. "But it's important. We had to warn him. After the gunfight the other night, the civic leaders of Animas City held a special meeting. They've posted the Kid. If he so much as set a foot in town, any citizen has the right and the blessing of the community to gun him down in the street."

"All legal-like," Clarice spat. "A friend slipped us news of the meeting in advance, and we went to have our say. But they wouldn't listen to us. Had us thrown out, in fact. So we chucked a rock through a window and lit out to tell Alonzo."

"We about turned back ten or twenty times," Wanda took up the account when her sister stopped. "Thanks to a rancher who saw you cross his spread, we found your trail and followed as best we could. Must have lost your tracks once a day, on average. But we plugged on."

"Then we lost them for good," Clarice continued. "We circled, doubled back, tried everything we could think of. It was no use. So we decided to go to the bottom of the foothills and pray we spotted you on your way down."

Fargo had no interest in hearing every particular, but they would not permit him to get in a word edgewise.

"About that time, the Utes found us," Wanda said. "We holed up in a wash and held them off for a while. When they outflanked us, we skedaddled."

"We were doing right fine, too, until my stupid horse threw me," Clarice lamented. "Sis tried to pull me up behind her, but the Utes were on us like wolves on a hurt antelope. They disarmed us and toted us here. What they have in mind, we can't say."

Wanda opened her mouth. Lunging, Fargo clasped a hand over it and rasped through clenched teeth, "Enough! You've wasted too much time as it is. We're leaving. Now." Brooking no dispute, he gave the Henry to Wanda, swirled Clarice into his arms, and turned. Outside, the hunting camp lay quiet. If only it would stay that way! he thought. Using a leg, he kicked the blanket aside and hustled from the lodge.

"Son of a bitch!"

Clarice's outburst was appropriate. Fargo halted, any hope he'd held of slipping away unnoticed gone.

Every last Ute warrior was waiting for them.

9

Fully half the Utes had arrows trained on Skye Fargo and the sisters. Fargo knew if he put Clarice down suddenly and made a stab for his Colt, all three of them would resemble porcupines before he cleared leather. Most warriors could unleash four or five shafts in the span of a minute. Once, during a friendly competition between the Crows and another tribe, Fargo had seen a young Crow perform the astounding feat of letting twenty arrows fly in that amount of time. So he made no unnecessary moves and warned Wanda, "Stand perfectly still."

Some of the Utes acted amused at the botched rescue attempt. The old warrior who had mimicked Wanda so successfully now imitated the squawk she voiced when Fargo started to dump her off his back. He had a fine sense of humor, this old warrior, but Fargo was not in a position to appreciate it.

Wanda sneered at them. "Come on, you vermin! What are you waiting for! We'll show you that white people know how to die!"

Fargo had met some cussed hardheads in his time, but Wanda Howard beat them all. "Speak for yourself," he said. "Better yet, don't speak at all. I want to get us out of this fix with our hides intact."

"What are you, yellow?" she responded. "You have a gun. Use it, for God's sake. We'll fight our way out."

"We wouldn't get three feet." Ever so slowly, Fargo lowered Clarice. She leaned against him, her hurt leg bent to keep the weight off her ankle. Holding his right hand in front of his neck with the palm out and his index and second fingers pointed upward, he raised it until the tips of his

113

fingers were as high as his head. It was sign language, specifically the sign for "friend."

The old Ute laughed. In a clipped, heavy accent, he said, "You speak with two tongues, white man. Friends not sneak in camp of friends. Friends not steal women from friends."

Fargo was not surprised that the warrior knew English. Some of the older ones had warmly greeted the first whites who penetrated the mountains. A few acquired a smattering of the language, enough to conduct trade, to barter and haggle. "These are my women," he stated. "You stole them from me. I am only taking back what is rightfully mine."

To Fargo's consternation, Wanda piped in with, "What the hell are you saying? We're not yours or any man's. Just because I fooled around with you in the barn isn't cause to claim me as your own."

The old Ute laughed louder than ever. He translated for the benefit of the other warriors, who shared his glee. "Maybe you speak with four tongues," the old Ute told Fargo. "Woman not want you. We keep."

Fargo glared at Wanda. "Now see what you've done? Keep your damn mouth shut, or so help me, I'll let them have you."

"Let us?" the old Ute said. "How you take them if we not want you to?"

"Think about what you're doing," Fargo said. "The whites in this territory will not stand still for having their women taken. They will send many guns against you. They will call in the army."

The old warrior sobered. "You think to scare us?" He gestured at the surrounding mountains. "This our land, our home. We fight if whites come. Kill many. And they never find women."

It was no idle bluff. In their remote mountain retreat, the Utes could hold off an army, if need be, indefinitely. As for the sisters, the Utes had explored every nook and cranny of their territory and could secret Wanda and Clarice where the best frontiersmen in the world could never ferret them out. Trying to intimidate the Utes into giving them up would not work. So Fargo resorted to another tactic. "Is this the new way of the Utes? To make war on women? Have you become like the Comanches, your enemies?"

"We make war on no one," the old warrior said. "Women on our land. We take as ours."

"As simple as that?" Fargo replied. "Then I guess it means that any time the whites find your women on their land, they can feel free to take them captive."

The old Ute grew thoughtful. One of the others addressed him and a debate broke out. Apparently some of them were in favor of handing the sisters over, while others were just as adamant about not doing so. Fargo gave them more to think about. "I know the Utes are brave. I know you would kill many whites if they send an army. But the whites would also kill many of you. Is that what you want?" He pointed at the sisters. "Are these women worth the loss of five warriors? Ten? Twenty?"

The argument became heated. Angry words and gestures were exchanged. Presently, the same tall warrior who had entered the sisters' lodge that afternoon now raised a hand and everyone else fell silent. The tall man spoke a while, whatever he said calming most of the others.

"Colorow say we hold council," the old warrior informed Fargo. "Decide what we do with you." He jabbed a finger at the Henry, then at Fargo's Colt. "Give guns. If we let you go, we give back. If not, we keep."

Wanda bristled at the notion, naturally. "Don't listen to him, Skye." She tried to level the rifle, but Fargo pushed the muzzle at the ground. "It's our only hope to get out of here alive."

Fargo stared at the ring of arrow tips poised to shear into their bodies. Paying no attention to Wanda's muttered curses, he wrested the Henry from her grasp and offered it and the Colt to the old warrior. He was sorry to part with the Henry. Rifles were highly prized by all tribes. The Utes would never give it back, even if they were allowed to depart.

Prodded by lances, the three of them retreated into the lodge. Two warriors assumed posts on either side of the entrance, while their brethren formed a circle around the charred embers of a campfire. As the blanket fell into place, Fargo saw the embers being rekindled. The council promised to last for hours. It promised to be a long, long night.

"This is a fine how-do-you-do," Wanda groused. Slapping his shoulder, she complained, "How could you be so dumb? As much as I despise the Durango Kid, I know he'd never pull the numskull stunt you just did. Now we're trapped. We can't fight our way out even if you grow a backbone."

Her insults were grating on Fargo's nerves. He was almost sorry they had "tumbled" in the straw. "Any time you want to commit suicide, go right ahead. Don't feel you have to hold back on my account."

Clarice came to his defense. "Don't be so hard on him, Sis. He's doing what he thinks is best to keep us alive."

"I'll ask the Utes to engrave that on his tombstone," Wanda said, then made a show of slapping her forehead and widening her eyes. "Oh, wait. Silly me. Indians don't use headstones, do they? Well, maybe they can carve it into his hairless head after they lift his scalp."

Fargo took a seat facing the opening. When would he learn not to stick his neck out for people who did not appreciate it? he reflected. His desire to spare the settlers in and around Animas City more suffering at the hands of El Gato had put his own neck on the chopping block. Unexpectedly, Wanda plopped down beside him, her shoulder brushing his. Unconsciously, he slid to one side.

"What? Do I have a disease?" she quipped.

"No. A mouth."

Wanda had missed her calling. She would do well on the stage in New York. Clasping a hand to her throat in exaggerated dismay, she said, "Don't tell me that you're upset over what I said? I didn't mean anything by it."

"Go around calling everyone a numskull, do you?"

"Sticks and stones, Skye. Sticks and stones. Sure, I could spit nails over what you did. And, yes, I do tend to say what I feel when it would be better to keep my mouth shut. But that doesn't mean I hate you or anything. I just think you were being an idiot. Hell, all men are. It comes with having your brains between your legs." She winked. "Nothing personal."

"I learn more about you every minute," Fargo commented.

"Ain't I a peach?" Wanda said, looping her arm around his and snuggling close. "Give me time, and I'll grow on you. Before too long, you'll change your mind about ever leaving."

Fargo wanted to kick himself. She had hoodwinked him, hoodwinked him good. Usually, he was able to gauge by a woman's personality whether she was the type to kiss and part friends or the type who viewed an intimate moment as an avowal of marriage. He tended to shy away from the second kind. Wanda had fooled him, had acted as if sharing herself was the most natural thing in the world to do, with no strings attached. She had not laid all her cards on the table. And he had fallen for her deception, hook, line, and sinker.

"Cat got your tongue, handsome?" she prompted.

Fargo did not mince words. Sometimes being brutally honest was the only way to deal with the situation. "When this is over, when I'm done with The Cat, I'm riding out."

Wanda squeezed him. "Sure, you are. But if you ask me, you're getting ahead of yourself. Before you can go after El Gato, we have to get out of the fix we're in."

Clarice was by the blanket, peeking out. "They're jawing something fierce," she reported. "That old one and the tall one are going at it like two curs over a table scrap."

"Maybe we should light a shuck while we still can," Wanda suggested. Turning, she pried at one of the poles. "We were aiming to break out before you showed up. I had a few of these pretty loose. Lend a hand and maybe we won't have to wait for the Utes to get tired of hearing themselves talk."

Fargo tested the poles she tapped. They were trimmed saplings, supple and pliant. Bunching his shoulder muscles, he slid the bottom of the first one outward without disturbing the others. One by one he did the same with a baker's dozen, creating a gap wide enough for a person to squeeze through.

Wanda poked him in the ribs. "See there? Men are good for something, after all. Besides giving a girl goose bumps, that is."

Fargo was beginning to understand why the older sister did not have a beau. She was a handful. Any man who took up with her had better have a hide as thick as an ox, or be deaf. Bending, he peered out. Four lodges were visible, but no activity was evident around any of them. With the warriors engrossed in the council, now was the time to escape. He hesitated, though. Running off might anger their captors. If the warriors gave chase and caught them a second time, there would be no convincing the Utes to release them.

Wanda jabbed him a second time. "What are you waiting for, big man?" she whispered. "Those heathens won't jaw forever."

Fargo had another reason for balking—the Henry and the Colt. He could always buy others, but he was loathe to part with them. The matter was taken out of his hands when Wanda ducked and dived out the opening as neatly as if she were diving into a pool. Clarice limped over and sank onto her knees. Extending her arms for Wanda to grip, she slid through. Partway, that is. She was brought to a stop when her dress was snared by the bottom of a pole, the fabric rending with a loud rip. All three of them froze, listening.

When no shouts rang out, Fargo peeled the dress free and gave Clarice a push. As he leaned down to follow her, footsteps sounded just beyond the blanket.

Fargo did not wait to see who it was. Scrambling out, he boosted Clarice to her feet, held onto her elbow, and made for the trees as fast as her condition permitted. Wanda stayed by Clarice's side, helping to steady her when she stumbled.

From the lodge they had vacated issued a wolfish howl. Someone had discovered they were gone. Now the entire encampment would be aroused. Fargo scooped Clarice into his arms and sped toward the black veil that blanketed the forest. If only they could reach it! The Utes were skilled trackers, but even they could not follow a trail at night.

Clarice clung to his neck. They passed one of the empty lodges, then another. The firs were twenty feet off when a strident yell heralded a chorus of yips and war whoops. Wanda, looking back, shouted, "Here they come!"

Fargo had to see. Five warriors were bounding in hot pursuit. Shoving Clarice at Wanda, he commanded, "Get her out of here." Then he whirled to delay the Utes. The fleetest was on him in moments, a war club hefted to bash in his skull. Sidestepping, he buried a fist in the warrior's gut, folding the man in half. Another Ute, carving a circle in the air with a Green River knife, was hard on the first man's heels. The blade slashed at Fargo's neck, missing when he pivoted. He brought his boot up into the Ute's groin, planted a solid right to the jaw, and ran for his life. An arrow nearly clipped his shoulder. A rifle blasted, his own Henry by the sound, but the shot was high.

Wanda and Clarice were nearly to the trees. A glance over his shoulder showed Fargo that every warrior was after them, plus the Ute women. He could not hold them all off. Wanda's headstrong nature had reaped calamity.

Reaching the sisters, Fargo grabbed Clarice to propel her into the woods. A shriek brought him around in time to dodge a tomahawk that would have opened him from his neck to his hip. Blocking a second blow, he drove his knuckles into the Ute's face. Cartilage crunched, and the man crumpled.

Other Utes were almost on them. Fargo stepped in front of Wanda and Clarice to take the brunt of the charge. He saw an arrow being nocked to a sinew string, saw an arm cocked to heave a lance. His own rifle was aimed at his chest. His own pistol was leveled. In another few moments he would be dead, and there was not a damn thing he could do about it.

That was when the undergrowth crackled loudly, and into the encampment thundered a zebra dun with an avenger in gray in the saddle. The Durango Kid did not slow down or veer. He rode straight into the Utes, bowling over four of them before the rest realized what had hit them. The onslaught scattered those who were in the dun's path, froze those who were too startled to think straight. Only the warrior with the bow kept his wits. Elevating it, he sighted down the shaft. But it never left his fingers.

The Kid drew, his ivory-handled Colt lightning in his hands. He shot the bowman in the forehead, shot the warrior holding the Henry, shot the one with the Colt, shot another who turned to flee. It broke the Utes and sent the women and a couple of the men into panicked flight.

A courageous warrior swinging a club leaped at the dun from the side, only to be blasted into eternity when the Durango Kid swiveled and fanned a shot that cored the warrior's throat.

Then Fargo witnessed something remarkable.

The Kid's pistol was empty. Now he reloaded, with a speed that was uncanny. His fingers seemed to have minds of their own. Fluidly, smoothly, incredibly quick, the spent cartridges were ejected and six new ones inserted. Fargo had never seen anyone do it so flawlessly fast, and he had met some of the best gun handlers alive. In two blinks of an eye the deed was done. Another instant, and the Kid dropped a warrior who rashly tried to transfix him with a lance, then fanned two shots in the direction of those who were fleeing.

Wanda hollered for joy and jumped up and down. Clarice had her hands clasped to her throat and tears of relief in her eyes.

Fargo stared at the dead and dying Utes, at the spreading dark stains, at a warrior gasping in vain for air. One clutched at his leg as he ran to the Henry. Wiping blood from the stock, he searched for the Colt. He found it lying partly under the body of the old Ute, whose blank eyes were fixed on his in ghostly accusation.

The Kid had hauled Clarice up with him. "I got tired of waiting, *amigo*, so I came to see what was keeping you. It is well I did, eh?"

"Wasn't he magnificent?" Wanda exclaimed. "Did you ever see anyone use a gun like he does?"

This from the woman who despised the Kid for courting her sister? "Come with me," he said, and jogged to a pair of horses tied next to a lodge. They shied, a bay going so far as to rear and flail its hooves. Taking the other animal by the rope halter, Fargo stroked its neck. "Climb on," he instructed Wanda. She complied, but much too slowly to suit him out of fear of being bitten or kicked.

Mounting behind her, Fargo hurried to the pines. "The Utes will rally and try to pick us off from ambush," he predicted. "Let's ride."

"*Sí*," the Kid said. Clarice's hand was in his, and he was beaming in joy, too lovestruck to realize the enormous implications of what he had done.

None of the surviving Utes sought to prevent them from leaving. Fargo assumed the lead, unerringly returning to the spot where he had left the Ovaro. Switching to the stallion, he hastened westward. Half an hour later he had not slackened his pace. They climbed the whole time, up steep slopes that would be hard to scale in broad daylight. At night, they were brutal. Logs and boulders impeded them. Again and again they had to detour around clefts and ravines. They reached the switchbacks that rose like wooded stepping-stones to the pass high above. Here Fargo drew rein and said, "We'll rest for five minutes. That's all."

Wanda had a protest to lodge. "What the hell is your hurry? I say we stop for the night right here. Lend me a blanket. I could sleep around the clock."

We're not stopping here, or anywhere. Not tonight. Not tomorrow morning. Not tomorrow afternoon."

"Why not? Did those savages put the fear of dying into you?"

Fargo glanced from one to the other. Clarice was exhausted, slumped against Alonzo. The Kid appeared content merely to have her back safe. Wanda was mad and confused. "Don't any of you understand what we've done? What will happen next?"

Wanda shrugged. "We killed a few Utes. So what?"

"So riders will be sent to every village within a hundred miles. The entire tribe will scour these mountains for us. Any outsider they find will pay for the blood we spilled. It could lead to war."

"Bosh. The mangy heathens wouldn't dare. They know we'd wipe them off the face of the earth," Wanda boasted.

Fargo had to remind himself that she was no different from the majority of settlers, that her attitude was widespread, even approved by the government. "Maybe the army will, maybe the army won't. We won't be around to find out if we don't reach the lower valleys before the Utes cut us off."

"How would they guess where we're heading?"

"They're not stupid, no matter what you believe," Fargo answered. "Warriors will be sent to watch the foothills and waylay any riders coming down out of the mountains. The Utes won't be satisfied until they avenge the loss of those the Kid shot."

Alonzo straightened. "Would you rather I had let them kill you?"

"No," Fargo honestly admitted. But it bothered him that his well-intentioned effort to end the slaughter of innocents might result in wholesale bloodshed. "You did what you had to. Now we have to live with it. The people in Animas City and on the farms and ranches must be warned."

Clarice stirred. "Alonzo can't go anywhere near Animas City, remember? They'll shoot him on sight."

"Then we'll warn them ourselves," Fargo said. Whipping the reins, he rode on. Whether they followed or not was up to them. He was tired of having every decision questioned, tired of being treated as if he were as green as grass.

For the next two hours they climbed one switchback after another. The wind bit at them in chill gusts, growing colder the higher they climbed. Its howl blended with the howl of wolves and the screech of mountain lions in a never-ending refrain. At night the peaks resembled stone castles. Those mantled by snow glistened dully in the starlight. The pass didn't come into sight until they were almost on top of it.

Clarice's teeth were chattering. "Lordy, I'm cold," she said. "Can't we stop and light a fire?"

"There's no wood," Fargo said. They were above the treeline, above the stunted growth that littered the upper slopes, above the rimrock, at the summit of the Rockies, on the crown of the world. Below, a sea of darkness stretched to a horizon blurred by the blue-black sky. So many stars lit the firmament, the spectacle took the breath away.

"Take my jacket, *querida*, the Kid said. Stripping it off, he helped Clarice shrug into it.

"What about me?" Wanda asked. "I'm cold, too."

"Hug your horse," Fargo advised. Pulling his collar higher, he spurred into the pass. Here the wind did more than howl. It shrieked. It screamed. It ripped his breath away. It turned his skin to ice despite his buckskins. And winter was months off yet.

Emerging onto a narrow ledge, Fargo came close to regretting his decision. A single misstep would plunge the stallion into oblivion, and him along with it. "Be careful," he yelled to be heard above the banshee wind. Hunching forward, he descended. Whenever a sharp turn appeared or slippery talus was underfoot, he warned the others. What had taken an hour to negotiate the day before now required three hours of constant concentration and expert horsemanship. That they all made it down safe was a minor miracle.

Once in the trees, they were shielded from the worst of the chill. Hooves pounded as the Kid brought the dun up next to the pinto. "Enough is enough, my friend. Clarice is freezing. We must stop, *por favor*."

The blonde was bent over, arms clasped to her sides, quaking like an aspen leaf in a storm. Her teeth chattered like the patter of hail on tin. "Please," she begged. "I can't go on like this."

All three of them looked at Fargo expectantly. He knew that if he refused, they would stay there anyway. "We'll rest until first light."

In record time the Kid had the dun stripped, his blankets spread out, and was under them with Clarice.

Fargo was in no rush to bed down. Shucking the Henry,

he hiked a hundred yards up the slope to check on their back trail. As unlikely as it was that the Utes had come after them at night, he sat on a log and studied the route they had taken, on the lookout for moving shadows. Twice his eyes played tricks on him, convincing him he saw skulking figures when there were none. Fatigue was taking its toll. Time to turn in, he mused, or he would be worthless the next day.

The rattle of loose dirt shook off the cobwebs that clung to his mind. He rotated on the log, sweeping the Henry up. From out of the brush walked Wanda, unaware of how close she came to taking a bullet. "It's just you," he said.

"Don't sound so glad to see me." Coming over, she sat and ran a hand through her tangled mane. "That wind made a mess of my hair. It will take a month of Sundays for me to brush the knots out."

"At least you're alive."

"Thanks to you and the Kid." Wanda put a hand on his shoulder. "I never did thank you properly."

"There's no need," Fargo said. He could not forget how she had treated him, or her comments about persuading him to stay on. "You should turn in. We'll be in the saddle all day tomorrow."

"I don't feel very tired." Wanda roved her hand to his neck. "I do feel cold, though, and I was hoping you could do something about it."

"No fire. If the Utes come through the pass, they'll see it."

Wanda slid closer, her lips puckered seductively. "It's not a fire I have in mind, handsome. I was thinking you could warm me up like you did in the barn."

Fargo thought she had been in the cold night air too long. In four hours they had to be on their way. What they needed most was rest. He was going to tell her that in no uncertain terms. But then Wanda did something that stifled the words in his throat, something that drained his will and set his loins surging. He could not have told her to go back down if his life depended on it.

She took his hands and placed them over her breasts.

10

Experience had taught Skye Fargo that females picked the damnedest times to wax romantic. They liked to claim that men were as randy as rutting elk, but if the truth be known, the fairer sex hankered after men just as much as men hankered after them. And when a woman was of a mind to share herself, then, by God, the man had better be in the same frame of mind or suffer her wrath. Never mind where it was or when it was, never mind what the circumstances might be. When passion ruled a woman's heart, the rest of the world was supposed to stand still while she gave her craving free rein.

Common sense told Fargo that Wanda Howard had picked the worst possible time. The Utes might show up at any moment. He should decline, he should get up and leave. There was always another day. But the delicious feel of her glorious globes under his warm palms set his blood to racing. Her touch ignited his lust. He stared at her ruby lips, at her crystal smooth complexion, at the baggy pants that hid her marvelous thighs. And he yearned for her with a hunger that would not be denied.

"What's the matter, handsome?" Wanda asked when he hesitated. "Don't tell me you're not in the mood?"

Fargo laughed, but it came out sounding more like a throaty growl. She smirked and pressed on his hands. Under his palms, her nipples hardened, becoming erect spikes. He tweaked one between a thumb and a forefinger, causing her smirk to turn into a delectable pucker. Squeezing her globes, he elicited a low groan. The pink tip of her tongue poked from her mouth.

"Ummmmmm. I'm warmer already."

Fargo pulled her to him and mashed his lips against hers. Wanda's tongue met his halfway. She sucked, inhaling him, her breath as hot as desert air in July. Their bodies fused at the hip and his hands roamed lower, massaging her flat abdomen. He swore that he could feel her stomach ripple to his touch.

"Keep going, lover," Wanda husked. "Keep going."

Happy to comply, Fargo dipped a hand between her legs. Automatically, they closed, trapping his fingers. She squirmed, somehow contriving to work his hand close to her core. Her legs parted when he lowered his lips to her neck and lathered her skin from her jugular to her ear. Lingering over the lobe, he rolled it with his mouth, then bit down lightly. His breath fanned her hair.

"Ah. Yes. Lordy, you're the best."

Practice makes perfect, Fargo mused, and undid a few buttons so he could slip his hand under her shirt. Swollen with desire, a breast filled his hand to overflowing. Exposing it, he shifted, his lips closing on the nipple. She was cream and peaches, sugar and spice, tasty and tempting. Her nails dug into his shoulders, and her backside slid back and forth on the log. Throwing what little caution he had left to the gusty wind, Fargo wrapped a hand around her slim waist and eased her to the ground beside the log, on the off-side, where they were protected to a degree from the chill. She ground her hips against him, firming his manhood. Preoccupied with her breasts, he was caught off guard when her hand closed on his pole and rubbed it from stem to crown. For a few moments he feared he would explode prematurely. But clenching his teeth, he mustered enough self-control to prevent it.

Fargo shifted to her other nipple. His right hand stroked her burning core through her pants. Wanda accommodated him by scooting her backside against his hand as if she were going to shimmy up his arm. His knuckles rubbed her knob and she moaned loudly.

"Do me, big man."

Not this time, Fargo promised himself. Before, in the

barn, they had been rushed. Now he would savor her as some men savored fine wine. He kept on licking and flicking her breasts, making her pant and wriggle, satisfying her carnal appetite in bits and pieces rather than in one quick gulp. For her part, Wanda ran a hand through his hair, knocking off his hat. Her nails dug into his shoulders, into his back. Somehow she loosened his gun belt without him realizing it and slipped a hand under his shirt to play with his ribs, running her fingers along each one in sensual stimulation.

Around them and above them whipped the wind. Trees rustled. Leaves shook. To the north a wolf gave voice to a piercing howl, every note vibrant in the high, crisp air. Fargo registered it all in the back of his mind. He had not let down his guard completely, nor would he, not with their lives at stake.

Suddenly, tugging at her pants, Fargo ran a hand underneath to the bushy thatch that guarded her dripping gate. He plucked at the hairs and wound them around a finger. Then, deftly, he plunged between her legs and into her tunnel. His finger was sheathed in wet silk. Wanda moaned again, a moan that went on and on, rivaling the howl of the wolf in duration if not in volume.

A burning ache formed in Fargo's loins. A lump formed in his throat. Undoing her britches, he worked them down, along with her underthings. Her charms were revealed to the world in all their pale, wondrous beauty. A musty scent tingled his nose. Gripping her hips, he knelt, touched the tip of his throbbing organ to her nether door, then buried himself with a savage thrust.

"Ohhhhhhhhhh!"

Wanda surged upward, clinging to him. Her lips were fiery coals, burning his chest, his neck, his mouth. She kissed him as if they shared the final kiss of all time and she wanted it to be indelibly branded in her memory. Her fingers locked onto the back of his neck, her ankles did the same at the small of his back.

Fargo commenced a rhythm designed to sweep them both to the brink. He did not care about the pebbles that gouged his knees, or the cold breath of the mountain on his back, or the dirt he was getting on his pants. His pulsing manhood filled her, stretched her, brought out the wildcat in her. For with each stroke she grew more animated. Her groans became louder. The speed with which they hammered one another quickened until the tempo of their slapping bellies was like the clapping of hands at a theater performance.

The world seemed to change hues. The black of night and the murky indigo of the shadows was lit by a rosy glow that came from inside Fargo, not outside. A glow engulfed his mind, growing brighter the closer they grew to the release they both sought. He was slamming into her with a vengeance, lifting her high with every thrust, when her dam burst and she gushed like a geyser.

"Skye! Oh, Skye!"

Wanda's thighs gripped him as if she would never let go and her nails bit deep. She also sank her teeth into his shoulder, perhaps to keep from screaming. For the longest while this went on, until she slowed and sagged, caked with perspiration. "My, my. You were magnificent," she gasped.

"Who says I'm done?"

Her eyes widened. She realized he was still rigid. At his next thrust, her eyes rolled back into her head, and she stuffed a hand into her mouth to stifle a screech. Holding her waist, Fargo drove into her with renewed vigor. Wanda lay as one dead for a few moments. Then her body galvanized into action, pumping against him almost fiercely. Her inner walls wrapped around his manhood like a velvet glove.

How many minutes went by, Fargo could not say. Lost in the delirium of sexual abandon, he was only conscious of the exquisite pleasure that coursed through him. Pleasure that built and built until every fiber of his being was awash in delight. He had the feeling that he could go on forever, that he would never find release. And, of course, that was when the release came. The lower half of his body seemed to rupture, to split down the middle, as he spurted into Wanda again and again.

"Uhhhh. Uhhhh. Uhhhhh."

She was tossing her head and smacking her lips and making a dozen different noises that blended into a single inarticulate groan. Her legs had gone weak, her arms were above her head. She was spent, exhausted, her eyes closed.

Fargo coasted to a stop, his own limbs momentarily weak, his lungs aching for breath. It had been incredible. He lay on top of her, cushioned by her engorged mounds, half inclined to doze off. Another bed of straw would have been nice, so they could sleep until morning.

The rattle of stones on the slope above put an end to his idle musing. Sitting up, Fargo groped for his Colt and found it down around his knees. Pushing off Wanda, he shifted. No one was up there that he could see. Pulling on his pants, he buckled his gun belt, then donned his hat.

Wanda stirred, dreamily regarding him through hooded lids. "Handsome, no one has ever made me feel the way you do. You drive we wild. Any gal ever mentioned how special you are?"

"Get dressed."

His tone snapped her out of her sluggish state. Sitting up, she covered her breasts. "What's wrong?"

Fargo scoured the upper reaches of the mountain. Shrouded in gloom, they hid their secrets well. "It might be nothing. Then again . . ."

Further prodding was unnecessary. Wanda dressed swiftly, brushing dirt from her pants and the back of her shirt. Once she was presentable, she turned to go. "We'll have to do this again sometime, real soon," she suggested, as sultry an invite as Fargo ever received. Sashaying like a dove in a saloon full of admirers, she descended.

Covering her, Fargo followed. He was ninety percent convinced that the wind was to blame for the noise he had heard. That other ten percent, though, kept him awake for another half an hour after Wanda turned in. The Kid and Clarice were deep in dreamland, the Kid snoring loud enough to be mistaken for an irate grizzly.

Morning came much too soon. It hardly seemed to Fargo that he had closed his eyes when the crunch of a footstep brought him up out of his blankets with the Colt out and cocked. But it was only the Durango Kid, who nodded.

"*Buenos dias, compañero. Tengo frio.*"

Fargo was cold, too. The brisk morning breeze sent an icy chill up his spine. At that altitude, the temperature would not climb into a comfortable range until the sun was well above the horizon. So Fargo's first order of business was to heat up some coffee. By using small pieces of old, dry wood, he kept the smoke to a minimum. Building the fire under overspreading limbs helped dissipate what little smoke did rise.

The heady aroma soon had Wanda on her feet, but Clarice was slow to rise. Stretching, the blonde tried to stand, only to cry out when her ankle lanced with agony. "It's worse than yesterday," she remarked.

"Do not fret, precious one," the Kid said, rushing to support her. "We will be in the saddle all day. Your leg will get plenty of rest."

Little else was said. All of them were eager to reach the lowlands where they would be safe from the Utes's retribution. After the animals were saddled, they climbed on and rode until the middle of the morning. By then they were thousands of feet lower, and the temperature was twenty degrees warmer. Alonzo was in good spirits. He whistled and sang and hummed, Clarice's slender arms locked around his chest.

Every now and again Wanda would glance at Fargo and wink. It did not take a fortune teller to divine why. When Fargo called a halt at noon to rest the horses, Wanda wrapped her arm in his and would not let go. Chatting merrily about anything and everything, she rubbed against him repeatedly—symptoms he had witnessed before. She was staking a claim, using her wiles in an effort to change his mind about leaving later on. He tried to think of a way to let her down easy, but there was none.

She had brought it on herself. From the outset, Fargo had made it plain that he was not sticking around. In all his travels he had never taken unfair advantage of a woman, never made promises he did not intend to keep, as some men did just to win a lovely's affections.

Once they were under way, Fargo deliberately hung back. Not only to fight shy of Wanda, but to keep an eye on their back trail. If the Utes were hard on their heels, he would know it soon enough. Twisting frequently, he surveyed the upper tracts, the barren slopes above the treeline. Along about two in the afternoon, as they crossed a sawtooth ridge, stick figures appeared below the pass—figures so high up they resembled ants, ants that filed into the open and wound lower along the route Fargo had taken. "I knew it," he declared.

The Durango Kid shifted to look. Clarice was napping with her cheek on his shoulder, while Wanda was a dozen yards ahead, immersed in thought. "How many hours behind us, do you think?" he asked softly.

"They'll overtake us sometime tomorrow morning," Fargo predicted. Now the big question was whether to stand and fight. Since spilling more Ute blood, no matter what the provocation, was to be avoided at all costs, riding hell-bent for leather was the logical alternative. There was only one problem. The Utes could go twice as fast. Even if he insisted they ride their mounts into the ground, it would delay the inevitable, not save them. As surely as the sun rose every morning, the Utes would catch them and kill them.

"One of us should hold the warriors off while the other gets the women to safety," Alonzo proposed. "There is nothing else we can do."

Fargo was not so sure, but he held his peace for the time being. As the sun arched lower and the shadows lengthened, he searched for a likely spot. By twilight he was still searching. In a glade watered by a small spring, he called a halt. The women were glad, but the Kid wanted to go on as far as they could while they still had some light left. "We can't waste a minute," he declared.

"It doesn't make a difference," Fargo said. "The Utes will stop for the night, same as us." Most tribes rarely fought at night. Some believed that the spirits of those who died would dwell in eternal darkness. Others believed the souls of the dead were doomed to wander as aimless specters. Still others did not fight after sunset for a very practical reason; warriors could not shoot what they could not see.

Even so, Fargo stood guard until midnight. The Kid took over after then. Nothing of note occurred, except the horses caught the scent of a mountain lion on the prowl and acted up until the big cat drifted elsewhere.

Morning was crisp but warmer than the day before. They were in the saddle before first light. Heavy timber slowed them, so much so that Fargo worried the Utes would be within sight by the middle of the afternoon. Toward noon, after they struggled through deadfall for over an hour, they found themselves on a sparsely covered spur with a cliff to the west, an open slope to the north, and more dense woodland to the south. Fargo promptly turned to scan the upper regions. He was so concerned about danger from above that he gave no thought to danger from below, not until Wanda called his name and said, "Look yonder. Who are those fellas?"

Fargo rode over close to the rim. A sheer drop of hundreds of feet ended among strewn boulders at one end of a serpentine valley. And there, crossing the valley from north to south, were eight men on horseback. Eight men, all wearing sombreros. Eight men, three of whom wore bandages on an arm or across a chest. At the exact instant Fargo saw them, one of the lead riders glanced up. The man bellowed, and the whole band drew sharp rein. One of their number spurred his animal a few yards nearer, shaking a brawny fist.

"We meet again, *gringo*! My fondest wish has been granted!" El Gato hollered. "Prepare to die, pig! You, and that *puta*!" His wicked grin widened when the Kid came into view. "So! The killer of my brother and his blond whore, as well. All of the eggs are in one basket." Barking orders in Spanish, The Cat spurred his mount toward the north slope. His men were quick to follow his example, a few snapping off shots.

Fargo reined to the north. "Into the trees," he cried. Lead clipped rock slivers from the cliff face, stinging their horses. The firing subsided once they were no longer exposed, but the hammer of flying hooves below was incentive to race for their lives. The Kid's dun, doubly burdened, was slowest, and fell behind rapidly. Fargo drifted back to watch over Clarice and Alonzo, as well as keep his eyes skinned for their pursuers.

The ground climbed at first, then fell steeply away and angled to the southwest. Fargo did not like being forced deeper into the mountains, but he had his hands too full negotiating the perilous slope to give it much thought. At the bottom, when he paused to check behind them, he was troubled to see that they had blundered into the wide mouth of a canyon. Towering walls reared on both sides. He cupped a hand to his mouth to direct Wanda and the Kid to go around, but Wanda was so far ahead that she was almost out of earshot. Spurring the Ovaro, he clattered in their wake.

For a while all went well. The canyon wound generally lower. Offshoots led up the side canyons, none of which had seen the foot of man in ages. Then the towering walls began to narrow, to close in on them. Bends were more frequent. Fargo tried to get Wanda and the Kid to stop, but they could not hear him over the pounding of hooves and rumbling echoes. Clarice glanced back, and he waved an arm to get her attention. She grinned wanly and returned the wave.

Yet another turn appeared. Wanda sped around it, then yelled something Fargo could not quite hear. The Kid vanished after her a second later, and tremendous squeals and whinnies pealed, mixed with oaths and a scream. Fargo slowed as he neared the bend, sparing himself the same mishap. They had collided, spilling all three riders. Wanda was dusting herself off. Alonzo had helped Clarice to rise and was ushering his sweetheart to a flat boulder so she could sit. He limped badly. Their horses were upright but shaken, the Ute mount bearing cuts and scrapes on its legs and flank.

Fargo gazed past them and frowned. It was a box canyon. The walls converged into a cliff twice as high as the previous one. No game trails broke the smooth surface, no hand or footholds offered an escape of last resort.

Wanda was in typical form. "Damn you, de Leon. Who taught you how to ride? I about broke half the bones in my body."

"Forgive me. I did not mean to," Alonzo apologized. "I tried to stop. There just was not enough room, or enough warning."

Fargo dismounted to examine their animals. Neither was seriously hurt. The same could not be said of the Durango Kid, though. Fargo saw him grimace and grit his teeth when he straightened his left leg. "How bad is it?"

"I can ride," the Kid said. Collecting the dun's reins, he swung on, but he did not slip his left boot into the stirrup. "We waste time again. Hurry. In this canyon we are like mice in a trap."

Wanda was fussing over her clothes. "I've heard of going from the frying pan into the fire, but this beats all. It ain't bad enough we have the Utes coondogging us. Now we have The Cat to deal with. What the hell else can go wrong?"

She should not have asked. For after they mounted and were hastily retracing their steps, four rifle shots rang out from the vicinity of the canyon mouth—a signal, of some sorts.

"We're cut off!" Clarice exclaimed.

"Maybe not," Fargo said. The canyon's half-dozen branches might offer a way out. Coming to the first, he motioned for the others to wait and galloped into the shadowy defile, a slash in the earth extending from the canyon proper much like the finger of a man extended from a hand. His hopes were dashed several hundred feet in when the offshoot did the same as the parent and ended in an impassable cliff.

"Damn."

Fargo hurried back. No additional shots had been heard, leading him to suspect the *banditos* were carefully working their way in. A frown and a shake of his head were enough to inform the Kid and the women what he had found. Riding swiftly to the next branch, Fargo moved along it at a reckless pace. This one was promising, at first. The walls widened, and the floor grew more open. But, on trotting around a twisting spire of rock, he learned that it was another dead end.

The sisters did not take the news well. Clarice had tears in her eyes and pulled at her bedraggled hair, while Wanda's curses were worthy of a sailor. Keenly conscious of the trap they had snared themselves in, they flew to the next offshoot, on the left. It narrowed, then widened, then narrowed again. The walls were close enough for Fargo to reach out and touch. Little sunlight penetrated, cloaking them in heavy shadow.

Nature tricked them once more. Around the final bend was a small cliff pockmarked by erosion. Fargo stared up at the top and commented, "It's not as high as the others."

"High enough," Wanda said bitterly, "unless our horses sprout wings."

"We try again," the Durango Kid said, wheeling the zebra dun.

But they did not get far. Northeast of them gunmen appeared, on foot, darting from cover to cover. The wily El Gato had made his men dismount so they could poke into every nook and cranny. "Quick. Out of sight," Fargo said, and trotted into the side branch before they were spotted. He passed the point where the walls widened, cantering into the narrow defile beyond. Here was the most easily defended position, and it was here that Fargo stopped and hopped down. Yanking the Henry from the boot, he took a position to the right of the gap.

The Kid came through next. He lowered Clarice, gave her the dun's reins, and dashed to a niche across from the Trailsman. "What do you want us to do, *amigo?*"

"We'll hold them off until dark. Then we break out." Fargo had to admit it was not much of a strategy, but it was the best they could do. Seeking to escape now, in broad daylight, would enable the *banditos* to pick them off before they were halfway to the canyon mouth. Outlasting the cut-throats was also out of the question. El Gato could send men for more water and food anytime. When they were weak from starvation, the butcher would breeze on in and finish them off at his leisure.

"That is your plan?" the Kid asked.

"If you have a better idea, let me hear it."

The Kid did not, but Wanda had something to say. "I have a notion," she crowed. "Why don't we wave a white flag? I have a towel that will do. We'll convince that fat bastard we want to weasel our way out. Have him come in under a truce, then fill him with enough lead to turn him into a sieve. With The Cat gone, the rest might leave us be."

Alonzo replied brusquely, "El Gato would never fall for so obvious a ruse. He is a *bastardo*, true, but he is not stupid. He will simply wait us out."

"I'm not hankering to die," Clarice commented. "There's got to be something we can do. Maybe start a fire and pray somebody sees the smoke."

She was so sincere that Fargo did not hurt her feelings by mentioning there was no wood. Or that the only ones liable to spot the signal were the Utes. He did say, "The important thing is we don't give up. I've been in tighter fixes than this."

"And you're still alive and breathing?" Wanda mocked. She regarded the rocky heights and snickered. "Funny. I never thought it would be like this. I never counted on dying in the godforsaken wild, miles from civilization. I always figured to die of old age, sitting on my porch in a rocking chair." She leered at Fargo. "Or in bed, with a smile on my face."

"Please," Clarice said. "Keep a civil tongue. A lady doesn't talk like that."

"I have news for you," Wanda said. "I'm a *woman*, not a lady. And I make no apologies to anyone." Wanda clapped her sister on the arm. "Hell, girl. It wouldn't hurt you to let down your hair now and then. You've always been a mite too prissy to suit me."

Clarice was shocked. "Since when? You've never complained before."

"Now is different. We have nothing to lose," Wanda responded. "All these years, you've been walking around with your head in the clouds. I never said much because I didn't want you to—"

The clomp of the zebra dun as it moved to the gap silenced them. Stupefied, they gaped at Alonzo de Leon, who had mounted unseen while they spatted.

Fargo shared their surprise. Straightening, he gripped the bridle and asked, "Where do you think you're going?"

"My angel must not be harmed," the Kid said solemnly. "El Gato is mainly interested in me. Perhaps I can lead him and his *pistoleros* off, give you a chance to slip to safety."

"It's too risky."

"But it's my life to risk." With that, the Durango Kid lashed the reins across Fargo's hand, causing Fargo to recoil. A jab of both spurs, and the dun was into the gap, streaking toward the main canyon. "Save my beloved!" were his last words.

11

"Alonzo, don't!" Clarice Howard wailed, and ran after the impetuous *pistolero*. But the dun was moving too swiftly for any of them to catch—not on foot, at any rate.

Swearing under his breath, Skye Fargo dashed to the Ovaro. There was no fool like a young fool, or no worse fool than a young fool in love. A tap of the spurs, and the pinto flew after the dun. Fargo intended to save Alonzo de Leon in spite of himself. But in the winding confines of the defile, the stallion could not attain its full speed. The dun had a sixty-yard lead Fargo could not reduce, try as he might. His anger climbed. The Kid was sacrificing himself needlessly. They were trapped, sure, but their predicament was far from hopeless.

Nearing the main canyon, Fargo heard a shout, then scattered yells, punctuated by a rifle shot. A pistol cracked twice and was answered by more rifle fire. The Kid had been seen, which meant he had broken into the clear and was heading for the canyon's mouth. Oaths and gunfire accompanied him. By the time Fargo reached the end of the narrow offshoot, a flurry of dust and dwindling figures on horseback were all there was to be seen. He started to give chase, then reined up.

The Kid had done as he said he would. Temporarily, at least, it was safe to spirit the women to safety. His sacrifice should not be wasted. And since some of the bandits might return at any moment, Fargo turned to fetch the women. The ring of horseshoes on stone spared him the task. Out into the sunshine rushed the sisters, riding double. Wanda drew rein. Clarice rose as high as she could to anxiously scan the canyon.

"Where is he? Why aren't you helping him?"

"We're getting the two of you to safety," Fargo said, and wheeled the stallion to lead the way.

"No!" Clarice cried. "We can't abandon him! El Gato will do terrible things to him if he's caught." She nudged her sister. "What are we sitting here for? Ride, damn you! Catch up to Alonzo."

Wanda shook her raven mane. "Sorry, Sis. But I have to agree with Skye. Your admirer has bought us the time we need. Let's light a shuck while we can."

Clarice was furious. "You never did like him!" she railed. "You've tried to break us up from the day we met." Hissing, she seized Wanda by the shoulders and pushed her sister from the saddle.

It happened so unexpectedly that Wanda had been dumped onto her side in the dust and Clarice was goading the Indian pony forward before Fargo galvanized to intervene. Flicking the reins, he brought the pinto alongside Clarice's animal and grabbed at the cheek-piece to the bridle. Clarice struck at him, crying, "No, you don't! I'm going to save him!" Fargo ignored a stinging sensation in his cheek and tried again. Succeeding, he brought her mount to a stop, earning a series of lashes and slaps for his effort.

"Damn it! Let go!"

Wanda came running up. Seizing Clarice by the waist, she wrenched her younger sister off. Instantly, Clarice tore into her, and the two of them went at it like wildcats gone berserk. Locked together, they tumbled to the ground. Emotions long pent up were released in a flurry of scratches and slaps and screeches. Wanda had her cheek opened. In retaliation, she wrapped her fingers in Clarice's blond tresses and pulled so hard that some of the hair was ripped out by the roots.

Howling, Clarice clawed at Wanda's eyes. They rolled this way and that, heedless of the grime they got on their clothes. Clarice's dress hiked up around her thighs, revealing creamy flesh. One of her breasts was partly exposed, but she did not care. Balling her fists, she walloped Wanda on the head and shoulders. In return, Wanda backhanded her.

Fargo checked the canyon. He was inclined to let them rip each other to shreds. But staying alive came first. Climbing down, he ran over and grasped the shoulders of the one on top. It happened to be Clarice. She whirled on him like a hellion and boxed his ear, making it ring. Pinning her arms, he said, "Calm down. This isn't the right time or place to settle old scores."

Clarice did not hear him. Livid, nostrils wide, she punched and kicked and even attempted to knee him in the groin. Fargo barely held on. He glimpsed Wanda, off to one side, watching in amusement. "I could use a hand here," he declared.

"Pistol whip the bitch," was the older sister's advice. "That should teach her."

Fargo resorted to a different tactic. He stomped his right instep down on her left foot. Clarice howled and bounced up and down, in great pain. "Now behave yourself," Fargo warned, "Or you'll get more of the same." Warily, he released her, raising both arms in case she came at him again.

Clarice came close. She tensed as if to attack, then her lower lip set to quivering and her eyes moistened. She was one of those who could cry at the drop of a hat, or quicker. "You're mean, just like her. You're taking Wanda's side because she gave you a toss in the hay."

"It was straw," Fargo lamely responded. "And it doesn't matter to me which of you kills the other. Just do it later, after we're safe, and the Kid is back."

The reminder brought a steady stream of tears. "Alonzo!" Clarice said in despair. "Where can he be? How can we help him?"

"By getting out of here," Fargo replied.

Contritely, Clarice let him steer her to the Ute horse. He boosted her up, did likewise for Wanda, and forked leather himself. No one challenged them as they sped down the middle of the canyon. The cutthroats were nowhere around, but Fargo found plenty of sign. Tracks showed that the Kid

140

had led El Gato and company on a merry chase into heavy timber to the north.

Fargo bore to the south. Thankfully, Clarice was too bleary-eyed from crying to see the tracks or she would have made a fuss over deserting her lover. As soon as they entered some pines, Fargo told the sisters to sit tight a few minutes. Scouting around, he discovered a recently felled limb with plenty of needles. Holding the long branch as if it were a lance, he rode back to the canyon mouth. Erasing their prints was simple to do. The trick would not fool a seasoned tracker, but few outlaws were expert at the craft.

Backing the Ovaro into the woods, Fargo cast the limb down. To be honest, it went against the grain for him to ride out on de Leon. But the circumstances being what they were, he saw no way around it. So for the next half an hour he put up with Clarice's blubbering and sniffling. In a gully hidden by vegetation on three sides and a hill on the fourth, he stopped. "This is where you'll stay until the Kid and I get back," he directed. Handing over the Henry to Wanda, he added, "If we don't show by morning, head for Animas City." A thought gave him pause. "You can find it by your lonesome, can't you?"

"I could find it in my sleep," Wanda boasted.

Clarice stopped snuffling long enough to say, "Wait. Take me with you. I can shoot. Just ask my sister."

Wanda did not wait to be asked. "Sure, she's shot a gun. But she can't hit the broad side of a barn at twenty paces. She'd be of no use in a gunfight."

Fargo had figured as much. "It's too dangerous," he said, and came up with a better excuse, one Clarice could not dispute. "Besides, I have to ride fast. Going double, we would arrive too late." Tapping his hat brim, he departed before she posed another objection. Halfway up the hill he looked back. They had climbed down and Clarice was crying on Wanda's shoulder. For all their spatting, they truly cared for each other.

On his own at last, Fargo held to a steady gallop until he reached the canyon. No one was there. Paralleling the tracks of the *banditos*, he forged northward. He had to cover four miles before he learned the Kid's fate.

Alonzo had been well in front of the outlaws when the zebra dun stepped into a deep rut. Mount and rider had gone down. Both had gotten up again, but the Kid's footprints were erratic, zigzagging every which way. The fall had dazed him. He had wandered aimlessly a score of yards.

El Gato's band had been right on top of him when the Kid came to his senses. The still-warm body of a bandit testified to the Kid's lethal ability. Somehow or other they had overpowered him and thrown him over the dun.

The trail pointed to the northeast. By the brisk pace El Gato had set, and the beeline the bandits made, Fargo speculated they had a certain destination in mind. El Gato must know the area well after hiding out there for so many years.

Intent on not losing the tracks, Fargo seldom took his eyes off the ground. So it was a stroke of luck when a nicker to his right alerted him that he was not alone. Pulling in close to a broad pine, he scoured the terrain. Since he was following the outlaws, he expected to see them. Instead, out of firs several hundred feet away came a Ute war party. Forty warriors strong, their faces painted, brandishing a host of weapons, they crossed a meadow and melted into the forest.

As if Fargo did not have enough to worry about. Allowing a couple of minutes to elapse, he spurred the Ovaro after the *banditos*. Adding to his haste was the prospect that the Utes might stumble on El Gato's trail and elect to wipe out the entire gang. It would be fitting, but not if Fargo and the Kid were caught in the middle.

Five more miles brought Fargo to the brink of a ravine. His initial impression was that the outlaws had gone right over the side, but closer inspection disclosed a cleft. A ramp composed mainly of talus led to the bottom. Fargo reined up at the top. Talus was notoriously slippery and noisy. The stallion was bound to create quite a racket.

Concealing the pinto in undergrowth, he cat-footed to the bottom. Loose dirt and dislodged stones rattled out from under him, but not enough to be heard any distance off. The bandits had gone to the left. Hugging the near wall, Fargo glided around boulders and past stunted growth. The acrid scent of smoke drew him on. It surprised him that no guards had been posted. But then, El Gato was as arrogant as the day was long. The Cat must think he was safe from reprisals. Fargo wondered if the bandit king would be so cocksure, and so careless, if he knew about the Utes.

Gruff laughter let Fargo know he was close. Crouching, he moved from plant to plant and boulder to boulder until the ravine widened before him. Slipping into a fissure in the wall, he set eyes on what no other white man had ever seen. It was a secret sanctuary of The Cat's, a crude cabin and spring and a long ramshackle lean-to under which supplies and saddles had been stored. Around a crackling fire were six gunmen, passing a silver flask back and forth. El Gato was not present, but the cabin door was open, and figures moved around inside. The zebra dun and eight other horses were tethered to the left of the cabin.

A few trees had taken root. Fargo did not pay much attention to them since they were of no consequence. Then he saw someone suspended from a limb in the deepest shadows. It was the Durango Kid, bound hand and foot, hung upside down by the ankles. His clothes, his sombrero, his gun belt were all gone.

As much as Fargo wanted to go to Alonzo, he dared not. To reach the trees, he had to cross fifty feet of open ground. Unless he could turn invisible, the killers would spot him and give him the same treatment. As he looked on, the cabin doorway was darkened by El Gato, who stood with his thumbs hooked under his bandoliers. In Spanish, the bandit king said, "Come, Bruto. We will amuse ourselves with our prisoner."

The biggest Mexican Fargo ever beheld walked out of the cabin, a huge man whose curly black hair lent him the aspect of a Hercules. Twin butcher knives hung from homemade sheaths. A serape covered shoulders as broad as a bull's, which was a fitting description of Bruto's facial features. The man lumbered on El Gato's heel, his soles thudding the ground as if he weighed a ton.

One of the gunmen by the fire saw The Cat and sprang erect. "Time for more fun and games, *amigos*. Let us see what El Gato has in store for the breed."

The Durango Kid tilted his head as his tormentors approached. "Tired of sitting on your fat backside, Joaquin?" he taunted in Spanish.

In English, Joaquin Hernandez replied, "Mock me while you still can, pig. Soon your mouth will be too swollen for you to speak." He strutted around de Leon, a cat toying with the mouse it had caught.

"Kill me and be done with it," the Kid said in Spanish.

Again in English, El Gato said, "And spoil all the plans I have for you, my enemy? No, I think not."

Fargo could not understand why the bandit king insisted on speaking English. Then The Cat gripped the Kid by the jaw and squeezed, violently twisting the Kid's face in the bargain.

"Remember what I told you earlier, half-breed? Use the language of the white bitch who gave birth to you. Not that of your father's country. You are an insult to him, to me, to all of us who call Mexico home."

"This from you?" the Kid spat. "From a murderer and thief and scoundrel who had to flee north or be executed?"

One of El Gato's men made the mistake of snickering. It enraged The Cat, who glared at the culprit, then hauled off and slapped the Kid across the face. The blow set Alonzo to spinning wildly. Joaquin Hernandez laughed heartily and nudged Bruto. "Look at him! The Durango Kid! The fastest *pistolero* who ever lived, some say. He does not look so fast now, does he, my friend?"

Bruto reached out to stop the Kid from spinning. His thick thumb and forefinger closed on the Kid's elbow. A grimace spread across Alonzo, and he bit his lower lip to keep from crying out. "Not fast," Bruto said thickly. "Puny, this one. I can crush with one hand."

"Not yet," El Gato said. "I want him to suffer. To suffer as I did when I heard he had killed my brother." The Cat smacked the Kid a few times. "Where is that glib tongue of yours now? Why are you so quiet?"

"Because I am holding my breath," the Kid responded. "I cannot stand to breathe the same foul air as you."

In the blink of an eye, El Gato's pistol was out and pressed against the Kid's temple.

Fargo heard the click of the hammer even where he was. Everyone stiffened in anticipation of witnessing the Kid's brains being blown out, but El Gato did not squeeze the trigger. Quaking with wrath, Hernandez slowly lowered the revolver, then smirked. "Nice try, de Leon. I came close. But it will not be that easy." Spinning, he roared at his men. "Do you hear me? Anyone who puts this son of a bitch out of his misery before I am done with him will regret it! I swear!"

"Relax, Joaquin," said a tall *bandito*. "We know how much you have looked forward to this. We will not spoil it for you."

El Gato grunted. To Bruto he said, "Begin. But do not forget what I told you. Do not hit his face. No broken bones. And he is not to bleed inside. Not yet, anyway."

The hulking human bear shambled to the Kid. Planting himself, Bruto delivered a powerful jab, the first of many, spacing them so that a few seconds elapsed between each. His knuckles were as large as walnuts, his muscles rippled like molten steel. It was an awful battering, a beating that turned Alonzo black and blue. The gunmen fell quiet. Only El Gato beamed, his eyes aglow with fanatical hatred.

Fargo yearned to step in. Every bruising *thud* of a mallet-like fist, every groan from Alonzo, churned his gut. But with the odds seven to one, he would be dead before he could do any good. He wished now that he had brought the Henry and left the Colt for the sisters.

El Gato let the punishment go on and on. Finally, he put a hand on Bruto and said, "Enough for now. We do not want him to pass out on us. Come."

The Durango Kid was in misery. His body was a mass of bruises and welts. His shoulders and calves were swelling up. Yet he shifted to face The Cat and said, "Is that the best you can do, Joaquin? Give him a club next time. Or, better yet, a rock. His fists are as soft as my grandmother's."

Before Hernandez could stop him, Bruto turned and rammed a punch into the Kid's stomach. De Leon sputtered and gasped, struggling to breathe. "Is that so, puny man?" Bruto said. Flexing his massive arms, he said, "Bruto is strong. Bruto is strongest there is."

The bandits drifted off. The tall one picked up a bundle lying near the fire and hollered in Spanish, "Joaquin, one moment, *por favor*. What about these?"

On the verge of going into the cabin, El Gato paused. "What are they, Ravera?"

"De Leon's clothes and gun belt."

"Burn the clothes. As for the *pistola*, smash it to bits. It is the gun that killed my brother."

Ravera was unhappy. "Begging your pardon, *patron*. But these clothes, this sombrero, they cost a lot of money. It would be a shame to have them go to waste when my clothes are so shabby."

"Ah, I should have known," El Gato stated. "Go ahead. Keep them, if you can bear the stench. But I meant what I said about the *pistola* and the *pistolera*. I want every trace of them destroyed." Pivoting, El Gato stepped through the doorway, then changed his mind. "No. Keep the pistol until tomorrow. I have an idea. Our guest will be quite hungry by then."

Ravera and others swapped puzzled glances. "You would have him *eat* it? But it is too big."

El Gato's grin was evil personified. "Guns come apart, do they not? Piece by piece by piece."

They were a sadistic bunch, these killers. Rowdy mirth filled the ravine. One of their number made coffee while another prepared supper. The shadows lengthened, dramatically so once the sun slipped below the rim.

Fargo was in no hurry to free the Kid. It could wait until nightfall, now that he knew El Gato did not intend to slay de Leon before morning. Safe in the fissure, he leaned back and rested. Moments later he was as startled as the *banditos* to hear a loud commotion from the direction of the talus slope. A horse squealed, as if it had taken a fall.

El Gato dashed out of the cabin. "Mount up!" he bellowed. "Go see who it is!"

Fargo felt he already knew. The Utes had arrived, and soon the ravine would be awash in blood. He pressed as far back into the fissure as he could as the outlaws swept past. Most had not thrown on a blanket or saddle, and rode bareback. After the fifth horse thundered by, he peeked out. El Gato and Bruto remained, the latter holding a rifle and stationed at a corner of the cabin. The Cat fingered his revolvers, as nervous as a cornered rat. For all his bluster, Joaquin Hernandez was a coward at heart, just as the Durango Kid claimed.

The blaze of gunfire that would herald a battle did not materialize. Fargo heard only loud voices and the clomp of hooves. All too soon, the gunmen returned. And they were not alone. One of them led the Ovaro. Another led a familiar Ute war horse—bearing Wanda and Clarice Howard.

Skye Fargo was mad enough to chew rope. The women had disobeyed. They had probably shadowed him the whole time, grown impatient when he did not reappear out of the ravine, and investigated on their own, bringing the stallion along in case he needed it for a hasty escape.

The Cat was thrilled. "Ladies!" he said in English. "What is it about me that you cannot keep away?" Clapping his hands, he crowed, "All my prayers are being answered. Maybe I missed my calling. Maybe I should be a priest."

Since being beaten by Bruto, the Durango Kid had not moved. Now his head rose, his eyelids fluttered. Appalled, he struggled at his bonds in helpless frustration. "No, no, no!" he cried. "Why did you come? Why did you not go when you could?"

Clarice vaulted off the dun and bounded to her man. Embracing him, she lavished hot kisses on his face and brow, then said, "What have they done to you? Oh, Alonzo." Pivoting, she took everyone by surprise by hurling herself at The Cat. Hernandez was caught off guard. Her nails seared his cheek, missing an eye by a cat's whisker. He retreated and tried to ward off her next swing, which slashed his wrist.

Bruto came to his aid, seizing Clarice from behind. Undaunted, she wrenched around and smashed an open palm against his ear. "Let me go! You're vermin, every last one of you!" The brute's arm compressed around her waist, and just like that, Clarice went limp. He dumped her at his feet like a sack of potatoes, then said, "This woman is puny, like her man."

The Kid thrashed madly, blood trickling from his wrists and ankles. "Do not hurt her!" he raged. "I swear, Joaquin, if you do—"

"What, breed? What will you do?" El Gato interrupted. "Spit on me? Call me names? I shudder in fear." Grasping Clarice by the hair, he brutally hauled her onto her knees. She was conscious, but stunned, sucking in deep breaths. "I could slit her from her throat to her navel, and there is not a damn thing you can do." A knife filled his right hand, the blade glittering in the firelight. He gazed down at Clarice a moment. "But I will not. It would be a waste, when we have been in these mountains so long with no companionship."

"*Sí, patron*," Ravera said gleefully. "Let us celebrate!"

Wanda had begun to dismount when Clarice charged The Cat, but a gunman had shoved a rifle against her ribs. Now, swatting the muzzle, she slid down and advanced on El Gato. "Get your filthy hands off her."

Hernandez shoved Clarice, who sprawled limply. "Tell me, *señorita*. What is it about *gringo* women that makes you think you only have to snap your fingers and men will jump to do your bidding? It cannot be your beauty, for most of you are as ugly as goats. And it cannot be your skill in bed, for the few Americano women I have raped were as stiff as scarecrows."

Ravera chuckled. "Was that before or after they were dead?"

Wanda squatted to shield Clarice. "Filthy perverts," she rasped. "If I were a man, I'd make you eat those words."

Fargo had his Colt out and trained on El Gato, but he did

not shoot. The women might be caught in the cross fire. He saw gunmen grab them and bind their hands behind their backs. Then they were dragged to the same tree from which the Kid hung, and tied to the trunk. El Gato supervised, caressing Wanda's chin when it was done. "Now what do you have to say, *puta?* Perhaps you want to beg me to spare you?"

Like a striking sidewinder, Wanda's head shot out. Her teeth clamped onto The Cat's thumb, shearing skin, slicing to the bone. Blood spurted. El Gato cried out and jerked backward, but Wanda was part snapping turtle. She would not let go. Two *pistoleros* leaped to their leader's side and pushed against her head to make her release him. She only bit deeper.

Again it was Bruto who knew just what to do. A single rap of a ponderous fist on her skull knocked Wanda out. Then Bruto wedged a finger into her mouth and pried at her teeth until they loosened. Scarlet rivulets trickled across her chin and down her neck.

El Gato held his hand to his chest, his thumb bleeding profusely. "This one is mine!" he bellowed. "The rest of you can do as you wish with the blonde, but I will take care of this witch personally."

Ravera hitched at his pants. "Now, Joaquin?"

"Later," Hernandez said. "After we have eaten." Stomping into the cabin with Bruto in tow, he slammed the door. His men ringed the fire and spoke in excited tones, casting lecherous glances at the sisters. The flask flitted from bandit to bandit, each savoring his share.

Fargo eased the Colt into his holster. For the time being, the women were safe. Wanda was out cold, but Clarice had sat up and was quietly weeping. Alonzo was in the grip of abject despair, his carefree soul crushed. Fargo took a gamble. When none of the bandits were facing his way, he partially exposed himself and waved to attract the Kid's attention, thinking it would bolster the Kid's spirits. But Alonzo did not spot him.

Ducking back, Fargo mulled over what to do next. He could not let the women come to harm. Whether he liked it or not, he had to confront the bandits. If only there were some way of cutting the odds, he reflected. A rifle left lying neglected would suffice. He scanned the area, but the only rifles were close to the fire, among them his confiscated Henry.

Long minutes went by. Fargo recalled the talus and considered pushing boulders down from the rim. Studying it, he suddenly felt as if an icy spear had lanced through his chest. On the west rim of the ravine, unnoticed by the *banditos*, lay someone who was spying on them, someone with a painted face and a pair of eagle feathers in his braided black hair. A new element had intruded itself.

The Utes.

12

Skye Fargo ducked back before the Ute caught sight of him. The warrior watched the bandits for a few more minutes, evidently taking note of how many there were and how many guns they had. Then he vanished into the gathering twilight. One moment he was there, the next he was gone, a human ghost who made no noise and left no sign to mark his passage. The unsuspecting cutthroats went on with their meal, joking and laughing, totally unaware of the savage doom that hung over their heads like the bloody axe of an executioner—an axe that might fall at any moment.

It changed everything. Fargo had been content to wait until the outlaws fell asleep before he made a bid to free his companions. But waiting was now out of the question. If the main war party was close by, they would attack before nightfall. That gave him half an hour, maybe forty-five minutes, to get them out of there before the Utes wreaked merciless vengeance. He had to come up with an idea, and he had to do it then and there, or the lives of the sisters and the lovelorn *pistolero* were forfeit.

But *what?*

One of the gunmen had produced a pack of battered cards and was dealing to a couple of others. A man with a scar on his chin cleaned his pistol. Ravera walked off, around to the rear of the cabin. Another stretched out and pulled his sombrero down over his eyes.

Keeping his back to the wall, Fargo slid from the cleft. Sometimes the only way out of a tight fix was to seize the bull by the horns, as it were, and hope for the best. The deep shadow at the bottom of the ravine hid him as he crouched and glided forward. Bearing to the right when the wall did, he froze when one of the cardplayers idly glanced up in his direction. His finger curled around the Colt's trigger, and he tensed to rush them, but the bandit merely yawned, scratched his armpit, and resumed play.

Cautious step by cautious step, Fargo circled toward the trees. The Durango Kid hung in limp defeat, his eyes closed. Clarice had leaned her head against the trunk and wept softly. Wanda glared at the *banditos*, her chin speckled by dried drops of El Gato's blood. When a grungy outlaw looked at her and smirked, she cursed him lustily. Laughing, the bandit picked up a stone and threw it. She shifted, but the rope hampered her, and the stone struck her shoulder. "You mangy polecat!" she raged. "Cut me loose, then try that. I'll gouge out your eyes!"

The *banditos* laughed at her antics. One mimicked her expression, and another cowered in mock fear.

Fargo was glad they were having so much fun at her expense. It made them careless. He was also glad they were seated close to the fire, a mistake no Indian or frontiersman worthy of the name would commit. The light dilated their pupils so their eyes could not penetrate far into the darkness.

Within ten steps of the trunk was a waist-high boulder. Halting beside it, Fargo switched the Colt to his left hand and slipped his right into his boot for the toothpick. Wanda had run out of swear words and bowed her chin to her chest. The bandits lost interest in her and quieted down. Fargo crept past the boulder, placing each foot down lightly. He had only gone a few feet when a figure came from behind the cabin and strode into the dim glow from the flickering fire. For a moment, he was rooted in place. The man's tall, slim build, the gray sombrero, the gray clothes, and fancy ivory-handled pistol—it was the spitting image of the Durango Kid. Then the man raised his head, and Fargo saw that it was Ravera.

Chuckling to himself, the *bandito* walked up to his companions and said in Spanish, "What do you think, *amigos?* Carmelita will swoon when she sees me next."

The man who had thrown the stone at Wanda now snickered. "I would faint, too, if anyone as ugly as you tried to kiss me."

Ravera did not appreciate the humor. "At least I have a woman, Gonzalo. The last time you were kissed by one was when you were in the cradle. And your mother never recovered."

Whiskey and insults did not mix. The man smacked down his cards and rose, saying, "You will apologize, Ravera."

Gunplay loomed. The others scrambled erect and scurried aside as Ravera faced Gonzalo. Fargo would have liked to see them kill each other, to cut the odds, but a bellow from the cabin doorway spoiled everything.

"Enough! Can't I leave you jackasses alone for two minutes? Anyone who causes trouble will answer to me!" El Gato stomped in among them, Bruto hovering at his side like a bushy-browed mastiff. "Speak up. Which one of you wants to have your spine broken first? Ravera? Gonzalo? Hector?" No one spoke. El Gato shoved Ravera, then jabbed a finger in another's bearded face. "How many times must I tell you? Get along together, or else. Anyone who does not agree is welcome to collect his share of the money and ride out."

No one offered to do so. Fargo back-stepped to the boulder, seeking to hide. Just then a gust of wind fanned the fire and flames flared, leaping high. The glare bathed the tree, the boulders, and him. Instantly, several of the bandits pivoted. Darting around the boulder, he dropped low to evade the volley sure to follow. But instead of the boom of guns, he heard throaty laughter.

"So. The last of the sheep has come to the fold. Stand up, *gringo*. Show yourself, or my men will put so many holes in the pretty *señoritas* that you will not recognize them."

Slowly, Fargo lifted his head. Every last bandit had a revolver pointed at either Wanda or Clarice. "Don't kill them," he said.

"Step out where we can see you," The Cat instructed. "I insist you join our little celebration."

Fargo quickly replaced the toothpick, then straightened, the Colt dangling from his trigger finger. They surrounded him as he stepped into the open. His arms were grabbed and roughly twisted. Ravera jammed a gun barrel into his ribs, sneering. "Let me kill him, Joaquin. You know how much I hate Americanos. We can tie him down and do like we did to that settler and his son. Remember?"

"No," El Gato said. "I have a better idea. He will provide us with entertainment." Hernandez clapped the hulking brute at his side on the shoulder. "We will let Bruto have him. I do so love the sound of breaking bones."

Without ceremony, Fargo was pitched to the ground near the fire. A ring of bandits formed, and into the ring lumbered Bruto. Fingers as thick as railroad spikes flexed and unflexed. Fargo heaved to his feet and backed away, angling to the right. The bandits had not given them much room in which to move about, which worked in Bruto's favor. For Fargo to evade him would be next to impossible.

The Durango Kid, Wanda, and Clarice were all riveted to the circle. Helplessness and misery racked them. For once, even Wanda had tears in her eyes. Fargo had been their last hope. His death would ensure their own.

Bruto sidestepped to prevent Fargo from getting past him. Flinging his huge arms wide, he inched closer. "Bruto kill you slow, *gringo*. Bruto break one bone at time. From there—" he pointed at Fargo's feet—"to there—" he pointed at Fargo's neck. "When Bruto done, you beg to be dead."

Fargo was unprepared for the swiftness of the killer's lunge. He had taken it for granted that Bruto was as ponderous as an ox, so he was caught flat-footed when Bruto's right hand closed on his left wrist. A violent tug crunched his teeth together, and he was flung into the air as if he were a child's rag doll. The world turned upside down. The bottom of the ravine became the sky, and sky became the ground. His breath was jarred from him by the impact. Dimly, he was conscious of cackling and chortling, of loud footsteps, of a hand closing on the front of his buckskin shirt and of being hoisted up.

Bruto's sweaty face eclipsed everything else. "You puny man, like Durango Kid," the killer said. "*Gringos* are all weak." He shook Fargo as a grizzly might shake a marmot, then dumped Fargo at his feet. "Get up, puny man. Fight me. This no fun."

Fargo pushed onto his knees. Matching his brawn against Bruto's was a lost cause. He had never met anyone so immensely strong. Craftiness was called for, the slyness of a fox pitted against the invincible might of a human mountain. Pretending to be more dazed than he was, he swayed and groaned. Bruto reached for his shirt again. At the very moment when those iron fingers touched him, Fargo exploded, slamming a fist into Bruto's jaw even as he surged upright and buried a knee in Bruto's groin.

The bandit staggered. Red in the face, he clutched himself, then sputtered and barreled at Fargo like a bull buffalo gone berserk. Fargo danced aside, only to have his arm snagged. He could not help crying out as his wrist was wrenched almost to the breaking point. "For that, you die very slow, *gringo*," Bruto said. He tried to grip Fargo's other arm, but Fargo would not hold still.

The other bandits were whooping and hollering, inflamed by blood-lust fever. "Kill him! Break his arm in half! Bend him over your knee! Rip out his throat!" all blended in chorus.

Exerting every fiber of his being, Fargo tore his arm from Bruto's grasp. He hurled himself backward onto the hard earth, his left hand brushing the flames. Slightly singed, he scuttled backward like an ungainly crab, Bruto plodding after him. He bumped against one of the bandits and was knocked onto his belly with the command, "Get in there and fight, stinking American!"

Fargo felt dirt under his left palm. Scooping it up, he flung it into Bruto's great moon face. Bruto blinked and retreated, swiping frantically at his eyes. Leaping in, Fargo delivered a flurry of blows that jarred Bruto, but did not make him go down. Smashing a fist against Bruto's taught him not to do it twice. The anguish it caused was worse than any pain it brought. He swept back a foot to plant his boot where it would do the most good, but lost his balance when a leg as thick as a tree trunk upended him. Spilling onto his side in front of his adversary, he looked up to see the sole of Bruto's left boot streak at his face.

He rolled without a moment to spare. Shoving off the ground, he brought up his fists, but was seized from behind by one of the *banditos* and propelled toward Bruto. An open hand cuffed him, almost casually, and he wound up flat on his back, staring up at a vault of gray filled a moment later by craggy features aglow with fury.

Bruto's face lowered. "You are mine now, *gringo*. It is over."

Judging by the cheers of the bandits, they thought so, too. Fargo let Bruto grab his shirt and let himself be raised. Bruto was drawing back a mallet fist when he stabbed the first two fingers of his right hand into the killer's eyes. Instinctively, Bruto released him and backed off. Fargo lowered his head and shoulders and charged. Ramming into the man's legs was like ramming into twin pillars, but he did what he set out to do and sent Bruto sprawling. Shrieks of outrage rose from the onlookers as they shouted themselves hoarse urging their champion to get up and finish him.

Bruto was in no hurry to heed. Blinking repeatedly, he slowly rose onto an elbow. He did not see Fargo spring behind him, but he reacted when Fargo's right arm coiled around his thick neck by jumping up and clawing over his shoulders at Fargo's sleeve. Fargo wrapped his legs around the giant's waist and clung for all he was worth while squeezing his arm with all his strength. He braced his left forearm against the base of the killer's skull for added support.

Bruto grew scarlet, the veins in his temples bulging. He wheezed with every breath, like a bellows losing air. Thrusting both elbows behind him, he tried to dislodge his tormentor.

Fargo held on. His rib cage was speared by agony, his arm was pummeled, his legs were pounded, but he clung on. Squeezing, always squeezing, he would not relent no matter what Bruto did. The giant became frantic, turning this way and that, beating at him in wild desperation. Of a sudden, the ravine fell silent. The onlookers had awakened to their champion's plight.

"Help him, you fools!" El Gato bawled.

Ravera and Gonzalo and others leaped to comply. But Bruto would not stand still long enough for them to do anything. In his mad thrashing and churning, he swatted them aside like so many flies. They tumbled to the right and the left, adding to the confusion. In the mayhem, no one could get off a clear shot.

Fargo gouged his arm deeper into Bruto's throat. Bruto gurgled and grunted, then tottered, flailing his arms. In his panic, the giant blundered into the fire and yelped as his legs were seared and the lower part of his pants began to give off smoke. Brands went flying. Stumbling into the clear, he doubled over to smother tiny flames devouring his legs. In so doing, he accidentally discovered the one means of saving himself.

Upended, Fargo momentarily lost part of his grip. Before he could compensate, Bruto twisted sharply and bucked like a mustang. Fargo's whole body shifted to the right. Sensing victory, Bruto bucked to the left, and down. Fargo slid farther, his head and shoulders dropping below Bruto's. Hands seized his elbow, his hair, and he was bodily ripped from his perch and thrown to the dirt.

"Get him!" The Cat roared.

Some of the bandits converged. Fargo, in rising, snatched a burning brand and swung it in an arc, scattering them. Only El Gato stood firm. Casting the brand away, Fargo pounced, his fist connecting with Joaquin Hernandez's jaw. The *banditos* would slay him, but he would not die alone. Death would be easier to accept if he put an end to El Gato's reign of terror. Hooking a foot behind The Cat's leg, Fargo tripped the butcher, then hiked his pants to draw the Arkansas toothpick.

A shrill scream froze everyone in place. It was the sort of scream that prickles the scalp and makes the short hairs at the nape of the neck stand on end—the sort of scream that chills the blood and lingers in nightmares for years to come.

A lanky bandit stood with his arms flung to the heavens and his face smeared with blood. Jutting from his right eye was the feathered end of an arrow. The barbed point protruded from under his left ear. His scream seemed to have no end. It rose to a piercing note as he performed a grotesque pirouette, sinking to the earth in a lifeless jumble of limbs, the arrow pointing upward, pointing at the top of the ravine, at the painted warriors who lined the rim.

The tableau was frozen while the scream lasted. When it died, the red men on high and the bandits down below came to life. Arrows whizzed in a steady hail. Bullets buzzed like hornets. Ravera, Gonzalo, and the rest sought cover, firing as they ran, the thunder of pistols and rifles deafening.

Fargo was completely forgotten. He had taken his eyes from El Gato for a few seconds, long enough for the devious cutthroat to dart toward the cabin. Fargo started to give chase, then heard Wanda shout his name. Rushing to the tree, he slashed at the rope, as all around them bedlam ruled. In the darkening twilight both the bandits and the warriors were finding it hard to hit targets. A shaft thudded into the trunk next to him. A stray slug clipped a branch overhead.

"Hurry, will you?" Wanda coaxed.

The strands parted. Fargo tore the rope off, then yanked Clarice to her feet. She moved to the Kid, hugged him to her bosom, and poured hot kisses on his brow and cheeks. A bullet whined perilously near. An arrow sank into the soil to their right. "Let me at him," Fargo said, but she would not listen.

"Oh, hell," Wanda said, and shouldered past. Clutching her sibling's arms, she pulled Clarice off de Leon. "Save the cow eyes for later, you idiot. We've got to get the hell out of here."

Fargo wrapped his left arm around the Kid's legs and reached up to saw at the rope. The *zing* of a bullet past his ear caused him to duck just as the knife sliced through. De

Leon dropped like a boulder, so much dead weight. Fearing the Kid had been shot, Fargo lowered him, only to see the Kid's mouth curled in a lopsided grin.

"Is this your idea of a rescue, *compañero?*"

The toothpick made short shrift of the rope that bound de Leon's wrists. Fargo propped the Kid against him, then turned. Wanda and Clarice were huddled low, Clarice with a fresh bloody crease on her shoulder. Beyond the trees, the ravine was filled with swirling gun smoke, frenzied oaths, and carnage. Two more of the bandits were down, one dead, the other convulsing and frothing at the lips. A Ute lay at the bottom of the wall, a third eye attesting to why. Of more immediate concern to Fargo were two prone horses, one feebly kicking and nickering, the other struggling to rise, but lacking the vitality. Arrows were to blame. Fargo suspected the animals had been shot on purpose, to keep the bandits from fleeing.

"Follow me!" Fargo said. Staying under the trees, he jogged toward the cabin. They must pass it to reach the string, and it would provide some cover. Guns blasted on all sides. The outlaws were fighting fiercely, but they were hopelessly outnumbered.

The Durango Kid was too weak to stand, let alone walk. Fargo had to virtually carry him. Running from bole to bole, the sisters clinging to his heels, he came to the last trunk. Twelve feet of open space had to be covered next, a killing ground where anyone who showed himself was liable to take an arrow. The Utes were well concealed, picking the *banditos* off one by one.

Fargo coiled to sprint to the cabin. He paused when a strange incident occurred, an incident he could not explain.

Ravera burst from behind a boulder, racing toward the horses. Fanning the pistol he had taken from the Kid, the bandit zigzagged to avoid the rain of pointed shafts. He was in the center of the clearing, near what was left of the fire, when the lower half of his body swept out from under him as if he had been bowled over by an invisible giant. Crashing onto his stomach, he howled and gripped his left thigh. From it stuck an arrow. Another shaft narrowly missed him, and he snapped a shot at the rim. No more were directed at him, though, after an unseen warrior shouted.

There Ravera was, easy pickings, yet none of the Utes finished him off. Fargo did not know what to make of it. Having more pressing concerns, he gripped the Kid and bolted for the cabin. An arrow brushed his shoulder. Another imbedded itself in the wall. He was passing in front of the building when someone stepped out of the doorway directly in his path. Unable to stop, they collided. The Kid cried out. The other man swore luridly and rose with a cocked pistol in a grimy hand.

It was Joaquin Hernandez, a bulging saddlebag slung over a shoulder. Fargo dived, tackling the bandit king. They tumbled about, trading blows. Somehow or other they rolled into the cabin. A chair crashed to the floor. A table was tipped over. Fargo heaved onto his knees and landed a pair of solid punches that would have rendered most men senseless. But El Gato lived up to his reputation for being tough. Absorbing the punishment, he gave as good as he got, landing powerful blows to Fargo's jaw and brow. Fargo blocked a jab and threw an uppercut. El Gato recovered and stabbed a hand at his revolver. Fargo's draw was faster. His pistol's barrel clubbed The Cat twice.

El Gato slumped, unconscious. Cocking the hammer, Fargo placed the barrel against the butcher's ear. This was it. The moment of truth. One squeeze, and it was over. Or was it? Suddenly, holstering his revolver, Fargo stripped off his gun belt, shirt, and pants.

"Have you gone plumb loco? What do you think you're doing?"

Wanda and Clarice had entered, Clarice supporting the Kid.

"This might save Animas City, and the life of every settler in the territory," Fargo answered. Nodding at the older sister, he said, "Help me undress The Cat. I have to switch clothes with him."

"What in God's name for?"

Fargo did not waste breath explaining. El Gato's garb was too baggy and short, but it would suffice until he acquired a new set of buckskins. He had been meaning to treat himself to a new outfit anyway, and had been putting it off. Donning The Cat's sombrero, he strapped on the Colt, squeezed his feet into his boots, and replaced the toothpick. On a peg hung a moth-eaten coat, which he took and draped over the Kid. "I'll take care of him," he told Clarice.

Outside, the battle still raged, but fewer shots were being fired, and the Utes were being selective about when they loosed arrows. Ravera had crawled to a boulder much too small to shield him, yet he had not taken another shaft. It confirmed Fargo's hunch.

"So what now, handsome?" Wanda asked.

"We make a break for the horses and ride like the wind," Fargo said. He looked at Alonzo, who grinned gamely. "This won't be easy."

"What in life ever is, eh?"

Fargo edged outdoors. Staying close to the wall, he sidled to the corner nearest the string. Another horse was down, a dead *bandito* partially under it, but the Ovaro and the dun were still alive. "On the count of three," he said, palming the Colt. He scanned the wall above the animals. Utes were up there, somewhere, just waiting for someone else to do what the bandit had done. "One." To the rear of the cabin sounded a thump. "Two." A yip on the east rim was echoed by one on the west. "Three!"

A warrior rose the instant they appeared, an arrow nocked to a bowstring. Fargo banged off a shot that ricocheted from the rock wall, forcing the man to drop down. Hustling the Kid toward the stallion, he was a few strides from salvation when Clarice screeched in terror. Whirling, he saw Bruto bound toward them from the back of the cabin, a machete raised for a fatal stroke. Fargo pointed the Colt, but Clarice blundered into his line of fire as she backpedaled.

Shoving the Kid at the pinto, Fargo leaped to save the blonde. She tripped, falling in front of him, and he had to jump to keep from trodding on her. The glitter of cold steel was all the warning he had that Bruto had swung. The machete struck his revolver, numbing his hand, and the six-shooter fell. He glanced up as Bruto waded in. Hatred blazed in the killer's dark eyes, hatred so intense that Bruto forgot about the Utes, forgot about the other bandits, forgot about everything except his burning thirst for vengeance.

Again the machete whistled through the air. Dodging, Fargo skipped to the left. Any notion he entertained of the Utes ending the fight for him were dashed when he glimpsed warriors who had risen from hiding places, but who made no attempt to interfere. Maybe they were amused at having two of their enemies battle. Maybe they were conserving arrows. Whatever the reason, they merely watched. So, apparently, did the other bandits, none of whom wasted lead on him.

Fargo was almost decapitated by a swing he had not seen coming. Bolting to the right, he abruptly ran straight at Bruto. The bandit had thrown back his arm for another try and could not bring the machete into play quickly enough. Fargo smashed into him. They grappled, Fargo grasping Bruto's wrist—or trying to. For, with a seething wrench, Bruto freed his arm and aimed a stroke that would have cleaved Fargo down the middle, had it landed. A half step saved Fargo's life and an uppercut bought him space to retreat.

Bruto did not seem to care about the Utes. He did not seem worried that he might be transfixed by arrows at any moment. Jaw muscles rigid, he clenched the handle of the machete and padded toward Fargo on the balls of his feet.

What else could Fargo do but retreat? He dared not take his eyes off the bandit, as he learned when he glanced around to verify that the women and the Kid had made it to the horses. A hiss, like frying bacon, spared him from having his right arm severed at the shoulder. Bruto did not give him a chance to recover his balance, but thrust in low. The rounded tip of the machete grazed Fargo's inner thigh. Spinning, he backhanded Bruto across the mouth.

The brute lost all reason. Howling like a rabid wolf, Bruto pumped his arm. Sizzling steel weaved a tapestry impossible to evade.

Fargo was driven backward. To his dismay, he bumped into the side of the cabin. He could go no farther. Bruto, sneering, gripped the machete in both enormous hands. The outcome was a foregone conclusion. Then Fargo snatched the sombrero from his head and flung it at the killer's face.

Bruto jerked aside without thinking. Fargo was on him before the machete could descend. A fist to the nose, another to the eye, a third to the lower lip, he drove Bruto back, briefly stunned but not gravely hurt, certainly not hurt enough to explain why Bruto's legs gave way and he pitched onto his knees.

Behind him Wanda held a rock the size of a watermelon. She had brained him with it, and blood smeared its surface. "Quit fooling around," she scolded. "Let's get the hell out of here."

The Kid was already on the stallion, Clarice was on a bay. Fargo sprang toward the string, his own momentum crashing him to the ground when the iron jaws of a trap closed on his ankle—a trap with four fingers and a thumb. Bruto yanked, pulling him toward the elevating machete. His own grasping fingers brushed an object all but forgotten. The smooth grips molded to his palm, and he twisted.

"Bruto kill!"

Fargo fired as the killer's broad shoulders bulged, fired as the machete began to descend. His third shot cored Bruto's neck at the same instant that the blade *thunk*ed into the soil. His fourth drilled the sternum, dead center. No man could live after that, yet Bruto somehow started to rise, his hand reaching for Fargo's throat. The last shot blew off the top of Bruto's head.

"Come on!" Wanda yelled.

Pivoting, Fargo raced to the stallion. The Kid slid back so he could mount. A lithe spring and Fargo was in the saddle, the reins in hand. War whoops broke out as he goaded the Ovaro into a gallop. Arrows commenced to fly. "Stay close to the wall," he advised, since it hampered the Utes, who were above them. But not those on the other rim. Shafts cracked against the stone surface, one nicking the pinto's ear.

As if that was not bad enough, some of the *banditos* opened fire to avenge Bruto.

Fargo bent low. They were running a gantlet of death, a gantlet no living thing could survive. What they needed most was a miracle, and it was granted to them by a most unlikely source.

Out of the cabin rushed Joaquin Hernandez, dressed in Fargo's buckskins. Weaving unsteadily, El Gato waved a revolver. "Stop them! Don't let them get away!" He took aim, but an arrow sliced into his right shoulder. Stumbling, he fired at the rim, and another shaft imbedded itself in the fleshy part of his lower back. The Cat shrieked, then scrabbled toward the cabin.

Fargo saw a stocky warrior sight down an arrow to finish El Gato off. A shout by another Ute gave the stocky man pause. Oddly, Hernandez was permitted to go back inside. Then the stallion reached the narrow portion of the ravine, and Fargo had to concentrate on the twists and turns. They were safe from attack so long as the Utes did not have warriors posted between the camp and the talus slope. In dread of another ash downpour, he scoured the crest. It was empty. At the slope he slowed down. Shale and dirt made the horses slip and slide, but they gained the top without an accident and headed to the southwest at a breakneck pace.

It was half an hour before Fargo felt safe in stopping. On a hummock covered by aspens, he drew rein to survey the countryside they had covered.

"They're not after us," Clarice exclaimed merrily. "We did it!"

Wanda was her usual skeptical self. "Why aren't they? What gives?" She glanced at Fargo. "And what was that business changing clothes? You could have gotten us all killed, dimwit."

The Durango Kid straightened. "You're the dimwit. Fargo was brilliant. It's what saved us."

"How's that?" Wanda asked.

"Didn't you see Ravera?" the Kid said. "The Utes could have finished him off whenever they wanted, but they spared him. The same with El Gato. Ask yourself why."

Clarice replied. Clapping her hands and squealing for joy, she said, "I get it! The Utes spared them because Ravera had on your clothes, and The Cat had on Skye's."

"I was wrong about the Utes," Fargo said. "I didn't give them enough credit. They never planned to wipe out every white they could find. All they wanted was revenge on the men they blamed for the deaths at the lake." He paused, and when Wanda still appeared to be confused, he elaborated. "It was late at night, remember? The ones who got away never had a good look at the Kid. As for me—"

Wanda snapped her fingers. "The Utes mistook Ravera for the Kid because he had on the Kid's clothes, and El Gato for you because he had on your buckskins and has a beard like yours. They'll torture those two later, won't they? Once the rest of the bandits are dead?" She smiled sweetly. "It couldn't have happened to two more deserving people. Sorry I misjudged you, handsome."

Skye Fargo suddenly felt tired, so awfully tired that he could curl into a ball and sleep for a month. The events of the past few days had caught up with him. But first he had to get the women home. An itch under his shirt reminded him of something else equally important—that new set of buckskins.

LOOKING FORWARD!
The following is the opening
section from the next novel in the exciting
Trailsman **series from Signet:**

THE TRAILSMAN #193
BULLETS AND BRIDLES

Kansas, 1860, west of Pawnee Rock,
a land where pounding hooves
and pounding passions turned greed
into hate and hate into killing . . .

"Trouble."

The big man with the lake-blue eyes spat the word softly as he listened to the night. Listening was part of him, listening, sensing, feeling. The night was heavy, with that ominous stillness that all too often spelled trouble of one kind or another. He had become a believer in harbingers, portents that chose their own time and their own way to send their veiled messages. His lips pulled back in a grimace as he leaned back against the red cedar and stared out into the stillness. Not even the soft scurrying of field mice or the chatter of fox broke the silence. With another soft curse, he shook away thoughts of harbingers and let his mind turn to anticipation.

It was, after all, anticipation that had brought him to the rich, Kansas plains. Anticipation had a name, Carol Harwood, a face of green-flecked, hazel eyes and sandy hair and a body of long, lithe electricity. The memories flooded over him again, Carol's long body entwined around his, her breasts pressed into his mouth, deep the way she liked. It had been that way between them from the very beginning, from the first time he'd broken trail for her Pa, Ed Harwood. Carol had wanted him at once and, as he found out, Carol usually had her way. They had been wonderful times, ending only when her Pa unexpectedly died. Carol decided to take her sizeable inheritance and move from Iowa. She'd wanted him to go with her. "I've been planning," she'd said. "There's big money to be made in horses."

"I'm no wrangler," he'd told her and they had quarreled, Carol bitter, demanding, using all her passion to convince him. But he had gone his way finally, yet Carol had stayed in touch, her letters arriving with the regularity of the seasons, asking, inviting, reminding him of fervid nights. Sometimes he wondered if she still really wanted him that much or she couldn't stand not getting her way. And now opportunity, work, and time had combined to bring him close enough to visit and he was still surprised at how strongly anticipation had taken hold. Good enough reason to turn away portents and harbingers, he told himself.

Skye Fargo finished his meal of cold antelope jerky, undressed to his underwear and stretched out atop his bedroll in the warm Kansas night. He closed his eyes and let sleep finally wrap itself around him as the night stayed heavy and still. But he slept uneasily, though he'd no idea how many hours had gone by when he snapped awake, instantly aware of the faint swooshing sound. Whitetails leaping through the air, he knew at once as he sat up and caught sight of half-a-dozen of the deer sailing by as though they were propelled by invisible springs. They were in the kind of long, sweeping bounds that meant they sensed a danger only headlong flight could answer. As they disappeared into the night, he saw the orange glow lighting the sky, distant yet not distant enough for the deer.

Fargo pulled on clothes as he saw the glow grow brighter and he leaped onto the Ovaro without pausing to saddle up. He headed for the orange glow, watched it grow deeper, redder, and he squinted hard. No prairie fire, he decided with a measure of relief. Prairie fires were quick to spread horizontally. These flames stayed in place, fed on something contained, and he swore as he urged the Ovaro faster. When he crossed a low rise the flames became clear, reaching skyward, and he saw the burning timbers of the house they consumed with almost gleeful abandon. The screams of horses came to him as he closed in and he saw the double row of long barns behind the house. Flames were licking at their edges as they leaped from the burning house, the horses screaming in panic.

Fargo reined to a halt and leaped to the ground, his glance taking in the long, fenced corrals that stretched from the barns. He was running, on his way to the barns, when he glimpsed the shape through the smoke and flame, a figure lying but a few feet from the leaping flames on what was once the porch of the house. He changed direction and ran toward the figure as he ducked away from a falling timber that toppled from the house. Reaching the figure, he leaned down and saw a young woman clothed in a gray nightgown. She was alive, the soft touch of her breath brushing his face. As he gathered her in his arms, he twisted away from another length of falling beam as he carried the unconscious young woman.

He put her down on the ground when he was far enough from the burning house to be beyond falling, scattering bits of wood and ember. He paused for a moment, saw that her breathing was steady, and noted the bruise at the top of her temple. She'd come around in time, he was satisfied, and he left her, raced toward the barns, where smoke now sifted into both rows. Spying the corral gates, he paused to open four of them before he ran to the side doors of the first barn. Pulling the doors open, he went inside and began kicking and pulling open stall gates, leaping back at once as the horses thundered past him out of the stalls and out of the barn. He did the same at the second row of barns, somehow managing not to be trampled. The fleeing horses did exactly what he'd hoped they would. Instead of running back into the barns as panic-stricken horses often did, they fled through the opened corral gates.

Fargo stepped away from the barn, aware that there was absolutely nothing he could do single-handedly to stop the fire that had begun to consume both barns. He started to go through the nearest corral gate when the shots exploded, one splintering the top of the corral gate inches from his head. He threw himself flat on the ground in a headlong dive as another three shots grazed him. Rolling, he came up against the side of the corral as he yanked the Colt from its holster and saw three men running toward him. Three more came up from the right side, he saw. He fired and two of the figures went down, falling into each other as the others scattered. But Fargo was on his feet and running, all too aware that silhouetted by the flames behind him, he was a perfect target.

He saw a water trough and catapulted himself through the air, landed behind it as more shots rang out, four of them thudding into the trough. He lay flat, crawled forward, and peered around one end of the long trough. The figures had spread out as they advanced toward him; he took aim, fired, and one of the figures spun as he fell. The others halted, started to back away, lay down a barrage of shots to cover their retreat. Fargo stayed down until the shots ended. He poked his head up and saw three figures reach their horses who were standing against a thin line of red cedar. But they weren't about to flee, he was certain. They just wanted greater mobility in coming after him again. He pushed to his feet and raced to where he had left the Ovaro; the young woman still lay unconscious on the ground. He leaped onto the Ovaro as the three horsemen came toward him. When he saw a small stand of black oak, he sent the pinto into it. He let the horse crash noisily through the oak and saw the three riders veer to charge after him. When they were into the trees, he swung one leg over the Ovaro's pure white back and slid from the horse.

The Ovaro went on and Fargo dropped to one knee. He

had the Colt raised as the riders charged after the Ovaro. He took the first down with one shot, then the second man who tried to veer away and found he was too late. Fargo whirled as the third horseman didn't follow. The third man started charging at him from behind. Fargo fired and realized his shot was too high as the horse hurtled into him. Diving sideways, Fargo felt the front legs of the horse slam into his side, flinging him upward and into a tree trunk. He gasped in pain as he fell to the ground and knew he was lucky the horse's chest hadn't bowled into him. He lay down and shook his head and tried to clear away the yellow and red lights that flashed inside his head.

Fighting away pain, he shook his head again and the lights stopped exploding inside him. He heard the sound of footsteps crashing through the brush and pushed himself away from the tree and managed to half turn in time to see the figure rushing at him. Fargo tried to bring his hand up but the man's blow swept it aside and Fargo felt himself knocked backward. He hit against the tree trunk, realizing the Colt was no longer in his hand. The figure in front of him grew clear for an instant and Fargo saw the man aiming a hard right at him. As he jerked his head sideways, he could feel the blow whistling past him and could hear the man cursing in pain as his fist slammed into the tree. Summoning up strength out of desperation, Fargo drove himself upward as he kept his head down. He felt the sharp pain as his head slammed into the man's jaw, sending the man backward and down. Fargo brought his head up. The man lay on his back, the gun still in his hand.

Fargo brought his foot down onto the man's belly and the man cried out as his legs came up, his shot going wildly into the trees. Fargo bent down and pulled him around as he brought his arm up to fire. Fargo's pile-driver blow came down on the man, crashing into his arm, driving it into his body just as he fired again. Fargo winced as the bullet blew the man's jaw off and the figure went limp. Stepping back, Fargo cursed softly, drew in a deep breath, and searched on the ground until he found his Colt. Holstering the gun, he rummaged through the man's pockets and found nothing to identify him. He straightened up and didn't bother to search the other two he passed as he walked to where the Ovaro had stopped.

They wouldn't have anything to identify them, either, he knew. But a new and terrible realization swept through him as he walked the Ovaro out of the trees. He hadn't come upon a fire caused by carelessness or accident. No cigarette left burning, no lamp overturned, no candle catching a curtain had set this fire. It had been deliberately set to consume everything, the house and anyone in it, the barns and all the horses. They had plainly just finished their ruthless task when he'd reached the fire. They had seen him get the horses out and had come back to get him, no doubt infuriated that he'd foiled at least part of their plan. The terrible enormity of it continued to grow inside him as he emerged from the trees and stared at the scene. The barns were burning down and only blackened, charred timbers remained of the house, smoke spiraling upward in a dozen separate whorls.

As he walked closer he saw the young woman where he had left her, but she was sitting up. She turned to him as he came up. "You've come around," he said and saw deep brown eyes round with dazed shock. He caught a hint of fear come into her eyes. "You were unconscious when I found you on the porch," he said. In the glow of the still-burning barns, he saw short, brown hair, a face with even features under the smudges of ash, a well-shaped mouth, even hanging open as it was. The shapeless gray nightgown hid the rest of her.

"You found me," she repeated, shock still slowing her reactions.

"Yes," he said. "I saw the flames and came by."

She swallowed, pulled her mouth closed, and he saw nice, full lips. A frown crossed her smudged, bruised forehead as thoughts fought their way through the shock still clinging to her. "Andy. Did you see Andy?" she asked, fear coming into her voice.

"Who's Andy?" Fargo asked.

"My best friend. My ranch foreman," she said. "His room's in the rear of the house."

"There's no house left," Fargo said gently.

The deep brown eyes blinked back at him. "Find Andy. You've got to find Andy. Oh God, please," she half whispered. He nodded and went past her along the edge of the smoking remains of the house, his lips drawn in a tight line. If Andy had been inside the house, he'd certainly have been burned to death, probably beyond recognition. Fargo peered through the wispy spirals of smoke and scanned the charred timbers that had once been a house. He saw nothing that resembled a body and doubted he'd have recognized one if he saw it. He turned to go back when he spotted the shape on the ground a dozen yards away. He hurried to the figure and saw a man clothed in a red flannel nightshirt, short gray hair atop a face that held at least sixty years in it. He leaned down and saw that the man was dead.

But not from the fire, Fargo grunted as he saw the three bullet holes in the red flannel nightshirt, each surrounded by a stain of darker red. The man had been fleeing the house when he was gunned down. Fargo cursed softly, rose, and walked back to where the young woman waited. She hadn't moved and there was still shock in her face as she looked up. "You find him?" she asked, the note of fearful hope in her voice cutting into him.

"He wear a red flannel nightshirt?" Fargo asked softly.

"Always," she nodded.

"I found him," Fargo said, and she stared up at him as the unsaid slowly sank into her.

"Oh God. Oh my God," she said, her hands going to her face. He waited and let her fight back tears until she finally brought her eyes back to him. "The horses?" she asked, her voice hardly a whisper.

"I got them out, all of them," Fargo said.

"Thank God. Oh, thank God," she murmured.

"I let them go out of the corral so they wouldn't run back inside in panic. They're all over the countryside by now," he said.

"We'll round them up," the young woman said.

"We?" Fargo questioned.

"My hands. They'll be coming back sometime tonight. Tomorrow they'll go out and round up the horses," she said and started to push herself up. He offered a helping hand and saw that standing, she was no more than medium height, although she looked shorter in the shapeless night-gown. Her deep brown eyes searched his face. "I owe you, real big. Who are you, mister?" she asked.

"Name's Fargo . . . Skye Fargo."

A tiny furrow creased her smudged brow. "I've heard that name. You the one they call the Trailsman?"

"Sometimes," he conceded.

"I'm Darcy Ingram," she said, holding out a small but firm, smooth hand. "This terrible night was no accident," she said gravely.

"I know," he said quietly and saw the surprise slide across her even features.

"They tried to kill me, too," Fargo said. "They wanted to stop me from letting the horses out."

"The bastards," Darcy Ingram spit out.

"They give you that bruise on your forehead?" he asked.

"Yes, but I didn't see anyone. When the fire started, I woke and ran outside. I never made it off the porch. Some-one was waiting and hit me," Darcy said.

"And left you on the porch for the fire to finish off," Fargo said.

"Everybody knows I give my hands Thursday night off. They just waited till only Andy and I were here," Darcy said.

"Why?" Fargo questioned.

"Because there are a lot of rotten, no-good bastards around here," she snapped. "It'll take too long to tell you, now. Let's talk tomorrow. Can you come back. I'd like you to."

"Guess so," Fargo said.

"I'll expect you. Now, I'll wait here till my hands come back later tonight," she said.

"What then? You're all burned out?" Fargo asked.

"See those hawthorns over there?" she said, gesturing to a small cluster of trees. "I've a cabin just behind them, use it for guests, mostly. I'll stay there till we've time to re-build. The bunkhouse hasn't been touched, so the hands will have their place," she said, and he found the long bunkhouse beyond the corrals. "I've a few things to wear at the cabin and I'll buy new things in town, later." Her hand reached out, pressed his arm. "I can't tell you how grateful I am to you, Fargo, but that's not the only reason I want you to come back."

"It might not be for a day or so. I'll be going to Foxville, first, then I'll be paying a visit," Fargo told her.

"Foxville's the only town near here," Darcy said. "You can't miss it."

"Good enough. I'll stop back soon as I can," Fargo said.

"Whatever's best for you. I'll still be busy rounding up horses. There are some sixty of them to bring in," she said.

"There's something else to clean up," Fargo said. "Six of them, three near the corrals, three in the black oak."

Her mouth tightened. "I'll see to it. I know just how I'll do it," Darcy said, her voice ice. He peered at her but her face stayed an expressionless mask. She went with him as he walked to the Ovaro and her eyes took in the magnificent jet black fore-and-hindquarters and pure white midsection of the horse. "That's a fine horse," she said admiringly.

"It is," he said and her hands came up, pressed against his chest.

"Promise you'll come back, Fargo," Darcy said.

"Promise," he nodded. She lifted herself onto her toes, a quick, impulsive gesture and her lips brushed his cheek.

"Thanks again, for everything. I'm not good with words," she said.

"That'll do," he said. Up close, her small nose had an up-turned pugnaciousness to it, he saw. Darcy was plainly an independent young woman and he pushed aside the questions about her that went through his mind. They'd have to wait for his next visit. He pulled himself onto the pinto and waved at her as he sent the horse into a trot. The acrid smell of burnt wood and drifting smoke stayed with him as he rode back to where he had left his bedroll. The orange glow no longer lit the distant darkness as he reined to a halt, slid from the horse, and pulled off his clothes.

He stretched out on the bedroll and the night remained still and ominous, he noted. But then harbingers and portents never just vanished. They had a way of clinging, staying on to remind one that they were never an end but only a beginning.